Box of Rocks

A Maggie Gorski Mystery

Karla Telega

Tart Cookies Press

www.telegatales.com

Dedicated with love to my parents,
Orrin and Kathy.
They always told me I was creative.
I hate it when they're right.

"I'll start by paying new author, Karla Telega the highest compliment I can give: in many ways, her writing reminds me of that of bestselling author, Janet Evanovich."

Norma Beishir, Bestselling author of Chasing the Wind

"One can only hope this is not her last, as the tale is simply delightful. One of the best things about this book is that it proves there is nothing boring about turning 55."

Fran Byram, Portland Book Review

"First of all, this book is absolutely hilarious. The descriptions and dialogue are hysterical. ... The characters are vibrant and come to life in such a way that you'll believe they are real people who the author simply observed and recorded."

Mike Saxton, Author of 7 Scorpions

"Move over Janet Evanovich, Karla Telega's new book surprises like an ACME anvil! ... *Box of Rocks* is a fast-paced, smartly detailed, and gut-bustingly funny mystery, and I really hope there's a sequel!"

Allizabeth Collins, The Paperback Pursuer

"Author Karla Telega does an amazing job with the characters--not just with the personalities she creates but also in how she adeptly intertwines their lives."

Leslie Granier, Reader Views

Published by
Tart Cookies Press / November 2012

Tart Cookies
Moncks Corner, SC
www.telegatales.com

Published in the United States by Tart Cookies Press

ISBN 978-0-615-72562-8

Bear

Andy sighted through the scope one hundred yards to the west, shifting his position slightly in the deer blind to get a better view. From his vantage point, he could just make out the mine entrance through the thin screen of trees separating them from the clearing.

"You reckon he's gettin' too close?" He adjusted his sights "One shot and I bet I can make him piss hisself."

His partner was scarcely more than a shadow in the gray haze of waning light. Even in the gathering dark, the contours of regular trips to the gym could be seen under his camouflage sweater. His voice was surprisingly light for such a large man. The smooth baritone was deceptively mild, but his words were charged with authority, even at a whisper. They held a subtle backwoods southern twang that no institute of higher learning could erase completely. "Hold up, Andy. We don't want anybody nosing around, but there's no need to raise the alarm just yet."

"He was in there an awful long time. Plenty long enough. What I can't figure is why anyone would go in there in the first place. What's he lookin' for?"

"Take it easy. He'll get the message that he's not wanted here soon enough."

Andy had his doubts, but when his friend spoke with such finality, he knew better than to argue, so he tried a different tack. "He's scarin' away all the deer and I'm not so keen on freezin' my butt off for nothin'."

"It's not that cold, and I've never known you to whine about the weather."

"C'mon, Bear, I can see my breath. Besides, we're losin' the light and you just drank the last beer. Let's go to Ruby's and warm up. We can try again tomorrow mornin'."

Bear was silent for a moment, then laughed softly. "A couple of good old boys in the woods, liquored up and toting rifles. That makes us quite the cliché, old friend. We'll fire off a couple rounds when we get to the truck, just to let the guy know he's not alone out here. Maybe he'll have the good sense not to come back."

Chapter One

"I feel like I'm supporting illicit Bambi trafficking. I'll never be able to show my face in children's movie theaters again." Maggie said.

Cher smiled at her. "Honestly, darling, I don't know how you can sleep at nights."

As Maggie rounded a curve in the driveway, the small house came into view. She looked around in dismay. The paint was peeling, and there was a definite bow to the porch roof, which foretold imminent self-demolition. Two sheds and four rusted-out cars littered the yard. She could swear that she heard pigs squealing nearby. Maggie stopped the car, took a deep breath, and put on her game face, striving to look as innocent as possible to the lovely people who lived here. She wouldn't want to be mistaken for a revenuer.

"I can wait in the car," Cher said as she locked her door.

"You are *not* leaving me to go in there alone! If I'm going to die for Ted's damn venison, I'm taking you with me." With an eloquent flourish she pushed the button to unlock all the car doors and slid out. She was immediately struck by the smell of smoke, laced with the heady aroma of roasting meat. *Heaven!*

She mentally went through her list:

Life insurance paid up: check

Will up to date: check

Wearing clean underwear: check

She was prepared for the worst.

As Maggie and Cher tiptoed onto the porch, a short stringy man appeared from around the side of the house. His sleeveless t-shirt was covered in dark red stains and spatters, and there was a bloody butcher's knife in his hand.

The women were poised to sprint back to the jeep.

"I suppose you're the lady who called me about the jerky." He wiped the knife on his shirt and pointed it toward one of the sheds. "Smokehouse is over there. You wanted a couple pounds? Do you want to come and pick it out for yourself?"

"Yes. *No!* I mean, no thank you. We'll just wait here on the porch."

Putting the lie to her words, Maggie stepped off the porch and began inching her way back towards the safety of the jeep, with Cher only a half step behind her.

As soon as the man disappeared into the shed, Cher turned to Maggie. "Are you out of your mind?" she growled. "I've heard what they do to women!"

It was like letting air out of a balloon. The nervous tension vanished leaving Maggie giggling. "Cher, *hee-hee* he seems very nice. How many times have you watched *Deliverance*?"

"Burt Reynolds, black leather vest, need I say more? Just remember, if we hear banjo music, we're burning rubber out of here."

"If we hear banjos, I'll run right over the top of you to get to the car."

The man reappeared with a bundle wrapped in butcher paper, and noticeably without the knife. Maggie composed herself, paid for the jerky, thanked the gentleman, and settled behind the wheel for the long drive home.

"I don't know why I let you talk me into these things." Cher scowled. "That could have gone very badly! He might have given you rancid meat, and then you're out twenty dollars. Whatever's in that package, I'm not going back there to exchange it."

"I thought you were more worried about your virtue."

Cher snorted and turned to look out the window.

Maggie thought about Cher's remark, *I don't know why I let you talk me into these things.*

Only a few years ago, Maggie had considered herself conventional, a rule follower. She had never struck out on her own, and rarely voiced her opinion. Lately, she had done a one-eighty, and found herself as the instigator for one misadventure after another. There wasn't any one defining moment that had triggered the transformation. She just didn't want to spend the rest of her life fading farther into the background. Cher had never complained about coming along for the ride.

At fifty-five, Maggie was already past hot flashes and irritability. She still had her looks. At least she was pretty enough if you took into account that she was ten pounds overweight, bowlegged, far sighted, and not a snappy dresser. She often felt a little awkward standing next to Cher, who was two years younger, two inches taller, and had curves in all the right places.

Cher was one of the sweetest people Maggie knew. In the six years since they'd met, Maggie never had known her to use a hint of profanity, and rarely heard an unkind word about others. It wasn't that Cher was pure as the driven snow. She had her share of vices, but then so did Maggie.

She lit a cigarette. Maggie knew that smoking was deepening the fine lines on her face, and was contributing to her osteoporosis. She quit smoking after she broke her shoulder in two places a few years ago. She had thought about using hypnosis, but when her father had tried that method years ago, he was left needing to pee every time he lit a cigarette. She settled for nicotine patches. One time, as she was checking out at the drugstore, the clerk asked if the patch actually worked.

"Oh yes. I've quit on them two or three times already."

After a year and a half clean, this last attempt ended when her beloved pet rat, Edgar passed away. He was pure white with blue eyes, blind from birth, and she loved how he would sit on her shoulder, making soft clucking noises in her ear. She stifled a sniffle now, thinking about him begging for popcorn while they watched old movies together.

Cher broke the silence. "Hey darling, could I have one of yours? I left my spare pack in my car."

"Help yourself." Maggie indicated the cup holder where the offending pack of cigarettes resided. She had switched from the more expensive brand when she quit her job and money became tight. A cloud of smoke and a flick of ash out the car window were her salute to the taboos of modern society.

"Do we really have to go to that damn book club meeting tomorrow?" Cher asked. "When we joined, I thought they were going to serve daiquiris while discussing Jane Austen. Somehow, we found the only dry book club in the county."

"Come on, Cher, we're going for the intellectual stimulation and thought-provoking dialogue. That's why we're reading *Pride and Prejudiced Vampires*." Maggie stuck her tongue out and made a gagging noise. "Oh, hell! Which of us wants to fake the Ebola virus to get out of it?"

"Your turn," Cher reminded her. "Last month I had bubonic plague."

"Yes, but the month before that I had terminal hemorrhoids. That should earn me a pass tomorrow."

Cher laughed. "That doesn't count. When you got your second opinion, the doctor decided that you just needed more fiber in your diet."

The book club was an attempt at a normal pastime—just something to get them out of the house.

Prior to that, their last ill-conceived adventure had been a trip to Scape Ore Swamp to look for a fabled eight-foot Lizard Man—whom they named Hal. Maggie had duly googled the location and printed up the directions. Unfortunately, once they got to the road indicated on their map, they could find no signs, or even a gift shop, to advertise the swamp's entrance. They finally parked on a small dirt road, undistinguished but for its lack of no trespassing signs.

On the initial sighting of Hal back in 1988, he reportedly destroyed the mirror of an unsuspecting station wagon with his three-inch talons. Maggie held out a perverse hope that her jeep would prove irresistible to the mirror mangler.

If Cher was reluctant to come with Maggie on that trip, she gave no indication of it. She turned up in a business suit and heels, packing a camera, a pad, and a pencil, ready to put her recently earned journalism degree to good use. *The National Enquirer* would pay good money for an exclusive story.

They found a wooden deer blind in the woods built circa the Revolutionary War, but upon trying to climb the rickety ladder, it sank two inches into the mud. That pretty much ended any thought of taking the high ground, and waiting for Hal to take the bait. In the end, Hal was a no-show, so Cher didn't get her story, nor did

Maggie have to explain a broken mirror to the insurance company.

Consumed by her thoughts, Maggie didn't notice that the car in front of her had come to a complete stop to make a right hand turn—a rather common occurrence for South Carolina drivers. She slammed on the brakes, throwing them both into their shoulder straps, but the jeep stopped just in time to avoid a rear-ender.

Maggie cringed, then stole a sheepish glance at Cher. "Are you alright?"

"Looks like all the pieces are still there."

Maggie sighed before asking, "Do you really feel like I'm dragging you around?" The question had been dogging her for miles.

"Absolutely! But you know that unless it's something life-threatening, like antiquing, I'm right there with you."

Maggie had to smile. "You *know* that having an aversion to other people's old crap is unnatural."

"Darling, collecting musty smelling bars of homemade soap isn't exactly natural either. How many bars do you have now?"

"How about those Yankees? I hear they're going to the playoffs, or finals...whatever you call it in baseballese."

Cher's bubbly giggle filled the car. "Smoothly done, Maggs. If it weren't for you darling, I wouldn't know what to do with myself."

"You're the wind beneath my wings, sweetie."

Cher took a long drag on her cigarette. "So, how are your therapy sessions going? Are you still seeing that teenage psych with the bobby socks and ponytail?"

Maggie wrinkled her nose. "Sally is still looking for that 'defining moment' in my past that first triggered the panic attacks. She doesn't even have a single ink blot. How am I supposed to get un-crazy without ink blots?"

Maggie had started therapy when the fear of having another panic attack became just as debilitating as the actual thing. She was desperate not to get to the point where she was afraid to leave the house. Hunting for Hal might have seemed like a strange way to confront her fears, but his talons were less frightening than the mall at Christmastime. Maggie felt claustrophobic in crowds, becoming more edgy with each person who jostled her.

She turned off at the next exit and they stopped for donuts. Maggie had no self-control where maple donuts were concerned, while Cher's weakness was the Boston Cremes. The shop was noisy and crowded, so they ate in the car.

"You know, Cher, that guy in the orange jacket was giving you the eye."

"The one with the plaid shorts? He was old enough to be my grandfather. Honestly, they don't make enough Viagra in the world! Besides, darling, that biker was pretty interested in you."

"I've only seen one man who could pull off braids in his beard, and that biker was no Johnny Depp."

"He did have an eye patch," Cher said. "That made him look kind of piratey."

"It made him look like he just had cataracts removed."

Maggie hadn't caught any cute young guys looking twice at her for a while. Crusty old men with more libido than brains seemed to be the order of the day.

They spent the remainder of the journey in their own thoughts, comfortable with the silence and each other's company.

As Maggie pulled into the driveway, Ted flew from the house before she could stop the engine. Without a word, her husband opened the back gate, grabbed the venison and raced back into the house.

"You're welcome," Maggie shouted after him. As they stepped out of the car, she asked Cher, "Do you have time for a cup of coffee before you head home?"

"No darling, I need to make sure that Buddy hasn't eaten another couch. Now that he's had a taste of microfiber, he's going feral on me. Yesterday I caught him stalking lawn furniture in the backyard."

Maggie hugged her friend and watched her climb into her car. She turned on her heel and went inside, where she found Ted in the living room.

" … fourth quarter and the Gamecocks are up by three points," Ted mumbled.

"That would have been a much prettier apology if you hadn't had a mouth full of jerky when you made it."

He didn't hear a word she had said. If he was this intense now, she didn't want to make a venison run during the bowl games. He would probably trample her and rush inside without noticing her bleeding in the driveway.

Speaking of which, she barely had time to brace herself when she heard the thunder of padded feet coming down the hallway. Fluffy kept conveniently forgetting that he was not allowed to jump up on people. She had bruises where the one hundred-pound Rottweiller had pummeled her with joy.

"Uh, oh! Who's been in the bedroom?" She rumpled his head and stepped back. "I bet you were on the big bed while Daddy wasn't looking." Maggie knew what she signed on for when she found him at the rescue organization three years ago, and never regretted the decision to adopt him. As he reached his nose to nuzzle her face, she could smell the poop on his breath. Time to rethink the "no regrets" thing.

Chapter Two

Paul Lakeland cradled the clay jar as he emerged from the mine. There was no need for his eyes to adjust from the gloom of the lantern-lit tunnels to the rapidly dimming landscape outside. He was somewhat surprised to see that the sun was setting, and looked absently at his watch. The interns at the University chided him for being absentminded, and he supposed there was some truth to that. It was quite common for him to become so consumed by his work that he lost track of time. He couldn't be bothered with the mundane necessities. His refrigerator was stocked with mayonnaise, some wilted celery, and three bottles of protein water. Cooking was very near the bottom of his list of priorities.

This magnificent piece of pottery was the culmination of a year-long dream. He had laid out his gridwork and painstakingly photographed, measured, and catalogued every pinch of earth he had moved while freeing the partially buried vessel.

Countless hours of study made him an expert on the local indigenous people … and a total failure at a normal adult social life. Paul supposed it said something about him that he was more interested in people long forgotten than the girl in his favorite coffee shop, whose name he could never remember. *Linda? Clarice?*

He looked across the clearing to the tree line, sneezed twice, then greedily sucked in the damp air, softly perfumed with loblolly pines and black locust trees. It was a welcome relief from the cloying dust clogging his sinuses and grating across his eyes for the last two and a half hours.

As Paul set down the lantern, his backpack slid off his shoulder and fell to the ground. He took the jar in both hands and squatted down to bring it near the lantern light, where he could study the striations on its neck. It was amazing to find a piece from this period that *had* a neck. It was surely the work of a master craftsman, which suggested a society more evolved than typical hunter-gatherers. This piece had to have been commissioned for someone of great wealth or influence within the tribe.

Now, as he reached down to pick up his backpack, the pot became off-balanced and began to slip through the fingers of his left hand. He immediately whipped his free arm around, caught the jar, and cradled it to his chest like a newborn baby. His heart skipped a couple beats.

"Good thing that the girl in the coffee shop didn't see that rookie mistake!" he thought. *Janet? Simone?*

Studying the Creek Indians of the southeast was a challenging task. Without a written history, he'd had to piece together stories from the oral tradition, passed down by countless generations.

Just as Heinrich Schliemann had used Homer's *Iliad* as a guide in locating the city of Troy, Paul combined several Creek Indian legends to find the mythical town of the Wind Clan.

According to legend, the Muskogee, or Creek Indians, had their origins next to the tan mountains that reached the sky, long before Eagle created the low country of black water. Then, the Master of Breath sent a thick fog to cover the earth, leaving the people to wander around blindly. They scattered about and formed clans. Paul believed this fog would explain the origin of the Great Smoky Mountains.

The Master of Breath took pity on the people and blew a strong wind from the east, clearing away the fog. The easternmost clan was the first to see the light of day, and became known as the Wind Clan. Paul theorized that before Georgia and Florida were settled, the easternmost clan would be at the junction of the low country and the foothills of the southern end of the Appalachians. He had settled on a site near the town of McCormick, about 30 miles northeast of Augusta, Georgia, on the South Carolina side of the Savannah River.

If this jar proved his theory, his doctoral thesis would amaze all the professors in the University of South Carolina's Archaeology department. Perhaps *National Geographic* would feature his find on the cover of their magazine.

He walked the short distance to his makeshift campground and set his lantern on the camp table. At twenty-six, he was still young enough to have a sense of invulnerability, so he didn't think twice about camping alone in the wilderness. Camping: that implied sleeping outside. He wasn't at all sure that he would be able to sleep tonight. His mind was buzzing with maize fields and hunting parties. Did this jar once hold something as exotic as fermented honey, or something as simple as water?

Ever since he was a kid and his Uncle Howard hid toys for him to dig up in his sandbox, Paul had been an explorer. Whether he was cracking rocks open to see what was inside, or pretending that he was on the Lewis and Clark expedition, he was always looking for something new to discover. On his fourth grade field trip to a real archaeological dig, he was hooked. From then on, there was never any doubt what he wanted to be when he grew up. The thrill of finding something that nobody had seen in centuries was intoxicating. Even the grunt work of recording and cataloguing stoked his imagination. Bits of tools and bone and pottery spoke to him, begging him to listen to their stories.

Paul's thoughts were interrupted by a crack of thunder. Before the echo died, a second crack shook the night. That's when he realized that he was hearing distant gunfire … not nearly distant enough. He shuddered and pulled his jacket's zipper higher, wishing that he had brought an orange hunting vest for the October opening of deer season.

Paul tried not to look like he was fleeing into his tent, which was silly since there was nobody there to notice his sudden anxiety. He knew that the flimsy tent walls would afford him little protection from a stray bullet, but he immediately felt safer inside.

He wrapped the jar in one of his rumpled sweaters and settled into his sleeping bag. His professors teased him for looking like he slept in his clothes, which was often the case. His short brown hair had waves where he had run his fingers through it one too many times. His amber eyes were partially hidden behind the smudges and dust on his glasses.

It usually surprised Paul when girls took an interest in him. His features: height, weight, build, could only be summed up as average. He was totally unaware that there was something exotic and foreign in his facial structure that made him GQ handsome.

Even though he had pitched his tent on what felt like solid rock, he stretched luxuriously. It was exhilarating to be out in the field where he was not constantly stooped over a magnifying glass. Ah, the glamorous world of archaeology. Maybe he could score a few points with the girls if he got a fedora like Indiana Jones.

Chapter Three

Dr. Samuel Peters rubbed his chin absently as he focused all his attention on the evidence before him. "This is a remarkable find, Paul! You say these symbols around the base of the jar would be consistent with those of the Wind Clan?"

Paul pointed to some squiggly lines. "According to my research, this would be the symbol for wind, and that one next to it is the sun. This other is the Muskogee symbol for man."

"So let me get this straight. It was one of the Indian legends that inspired you to select the area above the falls as your starting point—how did you make that connection?"

Lakeland's faculty advisor raised his startlingly turquoise eyes as he spoke. He was not that much older than Paul, and had only been an archaeology professor for three years. His fingers looked like they should be holding a basketball, but while his hands were large, his six foot slim frame carried little muscle definition. Nobody would mistake him for an athlete. One thing that all the department agreed on was that his accomplishments were exceeded only by his ambition.

Dr. Peters was legendary for finding unrecorded early European settlement sites, but he showed little interest in pre-colonization civilizations. It was one of the reasons that Paul had chosen the subject for his doctoral thesis. He wanted to break new ground.

"It was actually a combination of legends, sir. But the White Potato tale narrowed down the search area significantly. The intermarriage of European settlers with the Creeks put the matriarchal practice of the husband joining the wife's clan to the test. The children of these mixed marriages had no clan to call their own. This would have a direct impact on settlement patterns. The White Potato tale suggested that the clans hadn't settled in the low country at this time: the place of soft ground and black water. The area was considered inhospitable, with its snakes, biting insects, spiders, mud, and hungry logs."

"I'm guessing that hungry logs are alligators."

"Yes, sir. The women prayed for a solution for their disenfranchised sons, and were directed to go to the land of black water and find a potato plant. The plant would give the name of a new clan to the children, and provide a source of food forever. The story would suggest that the original easternmost settlement was not on the coast, as one would think, but inland at the falls."

"Have you found other supporting evidence for your hypothesis?"

"There are subtle patterns of regularly shaped remains of a settlement near the cave on the aerial photos back at my room. The area is too overgrown to tell from the photos if there's a central square, which would differentiate a town from a village. It looks like there is a burial chamber in the cave, but I didn't want to disturb anything else until we can organize a dig. Would you be able to review the grant request to make sure I didn't leave anything out? I don't think we'll have any trouble obtaining the funding for a formal excavation, even if it turns out to be some other tribe or village. We'll probably need some special permission for an easement through the mine shaft to get to the cave entrance."

Paul stopped to take a breath, but Dr. Peters interrupted his thoughts.

"Yes, yes. Just email me a copy and I'll look it over as soon as I can. It's in National Forest, so we'll have to petition the government. Since there will presumably be human remains, we'll need to have the county coroner clear the sight for excavation. I'd like to see the site myself before I sign off on the proposal. Tell me Paul, have you told anyone else of this find?"

"No, sir. You're the first."

"Be careful not to spread it around the department until we've concluded the formalities. These people will cut your throat for less than an Indian burial ground. Damn academia!"

"Thank you, sir. I'll find a safe place for the jar. Just let me know when your schedule permits and I'll take you out to view the site."

"We'll want to move on this quickly. I have some free time this weekend. I want to examine the cave thoroughly. I'll leave pacing off the village to you, but I'll need the measurements as soon as possible. A central square would go a long way toward validating your theory. We'd better plan on spending the night."

"I have camping gear if you'd like to just sleep out by the cave."

"That'll be fine. You said it's about a two-hour drive to McCormick? Let's say we meet here at my office Saturday morning at eight-thirty."

"Thank you, sir. I'll be here."

He hit his growth spurt much earlier than his friends, towering above them all. That's when they started calling him Bear. He had graduated in the top ten percent of his class, for Pete's sake, but the hated moniker stuck to him like hot tar among his childhood friends and family. They were content to live their small town lives in ignorance and poverty. Few others in the family had shown any signs of ambition, but they all knew better than to ask him for handouts anymore. It was one of the many reasons that he tried to avoid them.

He was still taller than most of them, lean and muscular from his time at the gym. He laughed about being one of those obnoxious men who knew they were handsome and used it to their advantage. Women seemed to find him easy on the eye, and there was never any shortage of them in his life. He was driven to excel in his field of work, but he also enjoyed his toys: fancy cars, top of the line clothing, and fine Cuban cigars, to name a few.

The morning after spotting the young man at the mine, Bear looked for his car at the trailhead and staked it out. He discreetly followed Lakeland back to the University District, where he discovered the man's identity. Bear could have easily hired a private detective to follow Lakeland, but he didn't want to raise any suspicions. It was better to keep watch over the young man without involving anybody else.

The Archaeology and Anthropology building was on the edge of the campus, across the street from a little park. He had been sitting on a bench in the sunshine Monday morning, pretending to read a newspaper for the last half hour, dressed in jeans and a t-shirt in an effort to blend in with the other students. The longer Lakeland was inside, the more concerned he became. Was the young fool blabbing about his discovery to anyone who would listen? Bear looked up to see him exiting the building, talking to a tall blond man. That was very bad news. He had Lakeland's name and address, but the blonde man was an unknown in the equation.

After following Lakeland home Sunday, Bear had returned to the cave where he found what he was looking for: a gridwork of small flags in the freshly turned earth at the far end of the main chamber. He knew the cave was here, uncovered during the blasting of the mineshaft. It just never held any interest for him, until now. The narrow entrance from the mineshaft emptied into a huge cavern, carved out over millennia by an underground river. The floor was littered with large rocks and boulders before reaching the smoother stones near what remained of the stream. Anyone foolish enough to explore would be entering a wild cave, untouched by trails, tours, or gift shops. The original entrance from the outside was probably covered by a landslide centuries ago, so that the only known access available now was through the mineshaft. Lakeland had conveniently slopped paint on the ground leading to this corner.

The flags meant one thing above all else: he was coming back. If Lakeland *was* preparing for some kind of archaeological dig, there would be others coming with him.

There was no sign that Lakeland had penetrated farther into the mine, so the vein of gold that he and Andy had found in the western shaft was still their secret. They had surreptitiously been digging out the gold for three months now. It was slow going, but by the time the vein played out, they would be rich men.

There was always the problem of amateur prospectors in this region, but they mostly stuck to panning in the nearby streams. The eight-foot chain link fence at the mine entrance stopped most of the curious from entering, and at least slowed down the teenage party traffic. How could Lakeland have known about this place? The mine had been shut down one hundred years ago, and even most of the townspeople were unaware that the cave existed. Lakeland had been very determined to get around the fence. He was quick to find the gap between the chain link and the rock wall.

Bear didn't like it. If he waited too long to handle the situation, he'd soon have archaeology students swarming around the upper mine area. He couldn't let that happen. Perhaps he would have to pay Mr. Lakeland a little visit tonight.

Chapter Four

"How does that make you feel?"

"Good Lord, Sally! You've been my therapist for almost a year and you don't know how I feel yet? Have you been paying attention to anything I've said?"

An absolute necessity in psychology was to be unflappable. Dr. Sally Ann Douglas fit that description to a tee. She prided herself on meeting every situation with calm dignity. If a patient came in wearing underwear on his head, she would merely note in her file that briefs indicated a more structured and pragmatic viewpoint than if he were wearing boxers.

She made a note, pushed her tortoise shell cat eye glasses back up her nose, and asked, "Very interesting, Maggie. Where do you think this hostility is coming from?" She knew that patients like Maggie had a hard time taking her seriously because of her age. Even though she was only thirty, she had seen enough in this practice to age her twenty years.

She had cleaned blood out of the carpet after a teenage girl, distraught because her boyfriend had left her, cut her wrist in this very room. The girl had dropped the box cutter and wept gasping sobs after making the deep gash. Sally had never seen that much blood before. As she wrapped her sweater around the girl's wrist and applied pressure, she really smelled blood for the first time … truly *smelled* it. Copper? That's what her favorite mystery novels would have her believe. After the paramedics had taken the girl off and she had done her best to clean the floor, she pulled out her coin purse and started sniffing some of the pennies. Curiosity? Shock? It was hard to say.

"Oh, you haven't seen hostile yet!" Maggie growled. Her shoulders slumped and she sighed in defeat. "You're still poking and probing at my childhood. I've tried over and over to tell you, my parents were the best. They taught me to be responsible, respectful, and caring. They just couldn't teach me to be brave. I feel like I can remember every failure in my life, from the first time I tried going solo on baking peanut butter cookies for my Dad, to my last panic attack."

"You think panic attacks are a personal failure?"

"Don't you? I close my eyes at night, and they play back in my head. Last night I dreamt about designer dogs again."

Shortly after she quit her job, Maggie had agreed to housesit for her nephew, Derek, for a weekend. Derek had not yet come to the realization that he was gay. The clues had always been there. He had an impeccable sense of style when he decorated his condominium in Mount Pleasant. His two Shih Tzus, Dolce and Gabbana, wore designer doggie clothes and had color coordinated rhinestone collars to go with their wardrobes.

Maggie had watched *The Dog Whisperer* often enough to know that Derek's male, Gabbana, was the dominant one, so she felt extra protective of Dolce during her stay. She was still smarting over the feeling of failing at her job, and felt she had been on the verge of a panic attack throughout the first night at Derek's place. At one point, she snuggled Dolce lovingly against her breast. "Don't worry little girl. I'll be your alpha and protect you from Gabbana." She was wondering all the while how she would pull that miracle out of her butt when she could barely keep her breathing steady. She was trembling violently as she rubbed the side of her face against Dolce's little head. If she was hoping for some mutual comfort, she didn't get it. Dolce started wiggling to be put down.

"I'm trying to protect you, you little mutt," Maggie whispered. Dolce had responded by snarling and truly fighting her. Maggie was stooping to put her down, when *womp*, Dolce landed a right hook directly in Maggie's eye as she writhed in her arms. Maggie dropped to her knees and clutched at her eye as Dolce slithered out from under her arm to the floor.

Maggie felt like she was drowning, unable to catch her breath between the sobs and the painful constriction in her chest. She was on her hands and knees, mentally measuring the distance to the phone. Dolce chose this moment to pee on her foot, while Gabbana started humping her leg. She tried to drag herself to the phone, with Dolce weaving back and forth in front of her, barking viciously. Gabbana was still determinedly holding on while pleasuring himself on Maggie's thigh. Maggie gave up and collapsed on the floor waiting for the panic attack to pass, occasionally shaking her leg to try to dislodge Gabbana.

For the rest of the weekend, every time she came near them Dolce snarled at her and Gabbana tried to make a play for a little romantic ankle action. She couldn't even get close enough to change them out of their t-shirts printed with the words "Cute little bitch," and "Cute little son of a bitch." Since then, foo-foo designer dogs and panic attacks had been indelibly linked in her mind. Even now, she felt her chest tighten thinking about it.

Sally said, "As long as you're trapped in your own head, your nightmares will have plenty of fuel. If you're going to ruminate, do it by choice, in a structured way. Have you read the book I suggested, by Jampolsky?"

"No. I found another of his books at a used bookstore: *Love is Letting Go of Fear*. I figured it also has 'fear' in the name, so it should work. I don't see any point in paying retail for introspection and self awareness."

Sally smiled. "You're probably right; it's a good book. I'd like you to journal while you read it. Bring your journal next week and we can share your observations. Have you been doing your positive reinforcement exercises and keeping up on your gratitude list?"

"What, giving myself a pep talk in the mirror every morning? When I first roll out of bed, my lower eyelids are resting on my cheekbones. It doesn't inspire me to look in the mirror and say, 'I'm beautiful and I can do anything!' I don't think the gratitude list is doing any good. It just makes me feel guilty that I'm still having problems in spite of all the good things in my life. I feel like I'm letting down the people who love me."

"As long as you remain open to change, you'll continue to make progress. It doesn't happen overnight, but one day soon you'll look back and realize how far you've come. Have you thought any more about finding a hobby?" she asked. "A hobby can be fun and rewarding, and it can give you a sense of purpose."

"Who's been telling on me? I'm still looking for a hobby. Cher and I have a date to do some brainstorming this week. I'm sure that base-jumping is not going to be at the top of the list. It falls somewhere below growing sea monkeys."

"I imagine that you and Cher can come up with something that will test the bounds of the legal system. At least it would get you out of the house and out of your own head. Why don't we talk more about it when you come in next week?"

"Oh, look at the time! Gotta run." Maggie rose to leave.

"We have five more *SLAM*...minutes."

Sally walked to the mini-fridge and pulled out an energy drink. She would just have to make believe that it was vodka.

When Maggie returned home, she found Ted standing in the garage, staring thoughtfully at his arch-nemesis, the lawnmower.

"Are you even going to try to start it, or is it playing head games with you?"

"Maggie, a little respect please. You mustn't rush an artist. I'm the Van Gogh of lawn care—suffering for my art."

"Just don't cut off an ear when you slip and the mower runs over you."

Ted was six foot one and weighed 175 pounds. He had a weight advantage and a longer reach, so it should have been no contest, but the lawn mower never got that memo. Maggie kissed him, walked through the garage to the laundry room door, then paused to watch the battle.

"Here we go." *whoosh,* "You can do it." *whoosh,* "That's my girl!" *whoosh,* "This time." *whoosh.*

With each pull of the cord, his face got a little redder. His short brown hair, peppered with gray, started to curl slightly, dampened by a thin sheen of sweat. Maggie couldn't bear to watch any longer. She went inside to start dinner before Ted's words of encouragement turned into something a bit more colorful.

Five minutes later, Ted dragged into the kitchen. He looked at her with big brown doe eyes and simply said, "Please."

Maggie laughed lightly and went out to the garage. The mower fired up for her on the second pull of the cord.

As Ted took the handle, she shouted in his ear, "That's okay, baby. You softened it up for me."

Maggie was just setting the table when Ted came in, tired but triumphant. He hadn't had time to clean up before dinner. With just the two of them it didn't really matter that his pant legs were covered with grass clippings and his t-shirt was sticking to his chest. He was normally casual scruffy cute; now he was only scruffy. His good nature had him smiling despite the humiliating beat down with the lawn mower.

He turned his smile to Maggie. She often complained about being overweight, but her lovely five foot six inch frame fit comfortably next to him when they embraced. He had seen old photographs of her with her original hair color, but she'd started coloring her gray roots before he met her. It was now a beautiful shoulder length dark blonde, curling softly at the ends. It framed her high cheekbones, which he attributed to her Finnish heritage. He loved the completely kissable curve of her lips and her warm green-brown hazel eyes. He loved her sense of humor and her passion in the bedroom. After seven years of marriage, he still got that pleasant tingling sensation along his jawline when he looked at her.

Ted cleared his throat. "Now that the lawn looks good, how about we invite George and Elena for a cookout tomorrow? Cher can come along. I might even cook a tofu burger for George." He shuddered noticeably. "Elena's a good kid, but eating a nice juicy steak doesn't cause her a moment's remorse. I have no idea how she ended up dating a vegetarian."

"I must have raised her wrong," Maggie said, "or maybe she's made it her mission to lure George to the dark side. Her father tried to turn me into a Stepford wife, but it didn't take."

Ted had no children from his first marriage, but he loved Elena as his own daughter. "I don't think she's going to try to reform George, and I'm just as glad that Eddie never succeeded in reforming you. You'll always be the natural disaster that I've come to know and love."

She stuck her tongue out at him. She would probably think of her snappy comeback after he was in the shower. *Damn!* Now she couldn't think of anything but Ted in the shower.

The ink wasn't dry on her divorce before she moved in with Ted. They had been dating for the last few months of her separation from Eddie Marsh. She and Ted seemed to complement each other perfectly. Where she was admittedly a little self-absorbed, he was generous. Where she was an emotional box of rocks, he was stable. He didn't smoke, and he rarely drank. He didn't even snitch chocolate chip cookie dough. The man's resistance to temptation was legendary, except where she was concerned.

Ted worked for a small architectural firm. Fortunately for their financial situation, the firm was doing very well. Summerville had been steadily growing since 1988, when it was carved out of neighboring voting districts. At that time, the town was singled out for its black majority population. The growth since then was providing more integrated neighborhoods, stimulating construction of new businesses, and insuring job security for Ted.

Their home in Summerville dated back to the 40's, purchased as a Sears "kit home". The original design had been a warren of tiny rooms. Ted had knocked down some of the walls and opened up the floor plan shortly after they moved in. The process had been chaotic, but left them with a great room, two bedrooms, a study, and a breakfast nook. Maggie loved the bay window in the kitchen area. It looked out on her favorite lilac bush, which was about the only landscaping element that she had managed not to kill. Fortunately, the wild flowers in her front bed grew like weeds. They seemed immune to her neglect.

Aside from a short stint at marriage years ago, Ted had been a bachelor all his life. His couch had seen better days when Maggie met him. The arms were chewed up, there were stains on the white (now gray) upholstery, and there was a permanent indentation on one side, where Ted normally sat to watch TV. It was, however, the most comfortable excuse for a piece of furniture that Maggie had ever seen. She was truly sad to see it make its one-way trip to the curb. Now she had her first-ever matching living room set. The overstuffed moss green couch and chair were selected for comfort and stain resistance. A fake six-foot bamboo plant stood majestically in the corner, and fake ivy mixed with ferns adorned her bookcase. She didn't have a live plant anywhere in the house, since they rarely stayed alive for long.

Maggie loved antiques, but had very little room in her house for any additional furniture. She contented herself by buying old bars of soap, which she regularly changed out in the bathroom: lavender one day, and glycerin the next. On Sundays she set out the rose petal soap in her favorite antique soap dish. As decorating went, it wouldn't make it to *Better Homes and Gardens*, but it made her happy.

Ted had never faulted Maggie on her hiatus from work. They had enough money to get by, and he had seen the debilitating effects of her panic attacks. She had held many jobs and felt increasingly inadequate at work, until her breakdown. A year of medication and counseling had helped, but the doubts haunted her. She wasn't sure that something as simple as a hobby was going to make a difference, but she was up for anything that would let her sleep at night.

She was finishing the dishes as arms wrapped around her from behind, and she breathed in the delicious scent of Ted's body wash. She felt the heat of his bare chest through her shirt as she leaned her head back against his shoulder. He leaned forward and brushed his lips against her cheek. A fine growth of stubble scratched deliciously against the side of her face and caught in her hair. She knew that a nice romp in the bed sheets didn't qualify as a hobby, but she suspected that a little physical therapy would help her feel better.

Chapter Five

That was just going to have to be good enough. After all, it was only family coming, so she didn't really have to wash out the toilets with boiling bleach. Maggie gave the kitchen sink one last rinse, just because she took childlike pleasure in using the sprayer. "Simple pleasures for simple minds," Mom would say.

She heard high-pitched yipping and knew that Fluffy would be bolting off the couch to meet Buddy at the door in 3…2…1…*bam!* Yep. He wasn't able to stop on the hard wood floor and ran head-first into the door. Fluffy would not be joining Mensa anytime soon.

Cher walked into the kitchen with two dogs bouncing circles around her. Buddy was eighteen pounds of rescued rat terrier, who could keep jumping four feet straight in the air for what seemed like hours. Cher could have taught Mother Teresa a thing or two about patience, or maybe she just didn't notice it anymore. Fortunately, Buddy also had an "off" switch, so most likely, he and Fluffy would soon be napping on the couch.

Maggie looked around her kitchen. She could have fit three of her houses into Cher's home in Coosaw Creek. Instead of a pool, Maggie had a creek in her back yard—during spring and summer. The rest of the year it was little more than a drainage ditch. She and Ted had wanted a small, one story bungalow in the old section of Summerville, and she was happy with her ditch. It was just a short walk to Azalea Park, where Fluffy regularly attempted to go after the giant tadpoles in the fishpond.

Cher was very well off after her divorce from Howard, a self-made man who bought and broke up companies for a living. She had the big house in a gated community, the cars, and a full-time housekeeper. Cher wore just the right shade of make-up to complement her blue eyes, and normally kept her long, bleach blonde hair in a stylish French roll. She rarely left the house without heels and a matching handbag and her nails were normally either bright red or icy pink. She didn't fit the usual job description for a super-hero sidekick, but then, Maggie couldn't see herself as a super-hero.

Cher had initiated her divorce twenty-six years ago, but the infidelity that had ended her marriage was Howard's alone. She never remarried and rarely dated. She was lonely and looking for direction in her life. That she would look for it with a depressed, neurotic soap collector like her was quite beyond Maggie.

Cher knew where to find everything in Maggie's little kitchen and she enjoyed cooking for more than just herself. Maggie knew better than to argue when her friend grabbed a bag of potatoes and started peeling.

"I thought you might make me some potato salad if I wished really hard. Yesterday I had to buy two pairs of larger size jeans, so I'm ready for anything. Bring it on!"

"You're beautiful the way you are, darling. Besides, I weigh more than you do, so quit complaining and pour me a glass of wine. I think that white wine goes best with peeling potatoes."

"When your stomach sticks out farther than your breasts, call me. Meanwhile, I have a fine vintage box in the fridge that hasn't turned yet, and you promised to help me with some ideas for my new hobby. I have a pad here, so we can start a list. Are we still in this hobby thing together or am I on my own?"

"Just try to stop me."

Maggie poured them each a glass of wine and started chopping the potatoes.

"Okay, Cher. I think the ideal hobby will have something new and engaging for me, and something worthy of a magazine article for you."

"A hobby is a fluffy golden retriever story, darling. Someday I'd like to write a big tough pit bull story. Dumpster diving for collectibles is amusing, but it's not investigative journalism."

"Dumpster diving is not going anywhere on the hobby list. I'd like hobbies that involve field trips farther away than behind the Piggly Wiggly. We need something that will get us out of the house, and that doesn't involve eight foot lizards."

"Our venison run yesterday was certainly evidence that some errands fall under the heading of 'surreal world.' Just for the record, I refuse to start scrapbooking, or crocheting toilet paper covers."

Maggie gave a chunk of potato to Buddy, who was milling around, looking for a handout. He pranced happily around the kitchen island and trotted away to the area rug before he spat it out with a look of disgust.

Maggie went to retrieve the offending object, and Buddy followed her back to the kitchen to resume his begging.

Ted yelled from the garage, "Maggie, do you know where the charcoal briquettes are?"

"They're leaning up in the corner near the garage door. That would be the corner with the spider the size of Old Yeller."

Maggie heard a muffled shriek, followed by what sounded like Flamenco dancing.

"Got it, thanks."

Cher put the potatoes to boil, put a couple eggs to boil in a separate pot, and they headed to the picnic table out back to have a smoke. Since summer had ended, the days were now in the seventies. Thunderstorms were becoming a thing of the past, so the creek was back to a drainage ditch. Thankfully, the dogs didn't feel the need to splash around in the water while they played in the yard. Maggie's sofa would thank her for that later.

Ted's luck with grills was little better than his skill with lawn mowers, but he would be damned before he asked for help. He had just gotten the coals going without singeing his eyebrows, when they heard a shout from inside the house.

The dogs were running for the back door at about Mach 2 as Elena and George stepped outside.

"Hi, kids!" Maggie called over the chaos of joyful doggie abandon.

"Hi, Mom! Your potatoes were boiling over so I turned them down. Are you making your potato salad, Cher?"

At twenty-seven, Elena Marsh was taller than her mother, and carried the "gorgeous" genes from Maggie's ex. She had eyes the color of amber and long wavy brown super model hair that always seemed to flow seductively in the wind, no matter which way the wind was blowing. She wore jean shorts that showed off Vargas Girl legs. After getting her MBA, she took over management of two family owned hotels in downtown Charleston. They were small, intimate and breathtaking; often visited by the rich and famous. Maggie would have to go without groceries for three weeks in order to spend one night at Hydrangea House.

When Elena turned thirteen, she was interested in learning more about her horoscope. Maggie took her to visit an astrologer, and Elena was hooked immediately. That had inevitably led to Tarot Cards and palm reading. Elena wouldn't think of making any major decisions now without consulting a psychic. She had different horoscope sites bookmarked on her computer, and an app for her iphone.

George lit one of his clove cigarettes and joined Maggie and Cher at the bench. He had recently started smoking them as a means of bonding with Maggie. She didn't know how he could stand the cloying incense smell.

"George, could you move downwind, sweetie?" Maggie asked. "You're interfering with all my toxins and carcinogens."

George seemed to be grateful for an excuse to put out the noxious cigarette. "Do you have any iced tea made up?" he asked.

"There's some in the fridge. Help yourself."

George was a good match for Elena. He was a Pisces with a slight overbite, whose palm lines showed virility with a sensitive side. Their personalities were polar opposites, but it worked for them. Where she was driven, he was easygoing. He was the same height as she was, with thick black hair and brown eyes. He looked slim, casual, and young boyish, if you didn't know about the muscles under his bowling shirt. At twenty-eight he already managed a bustling Piggly Wiggly in West Ashley. His only weakness there was when it came to hiring and firing workers. He was a sucker for a sob story.

"George," Maggie called, "could you please bring the plate of burgers from the refrigerator? The pale, diseased looking one is your veggie burger."

"Way to sell it!" George brought out the burgers, then helped Ted look thoughtfully at the charcoal as it heated. Cher dragged Elena and Maggie into the kitchen so they could talk while she finished the potato salad.

"I guess we should get started on this damn list. We could do something culturally and historically significant for a hobby, but a little on the weird side." Maggie began.

Elena snorted. "If it's not weird enough when you start, it will be by the time you and Cher are done with it."

"I'm sorry, darling," Cher said, "but I can't see us becoming tour guides at one of the plantations. You would probably forget your lines and just start making stuff up."

"You're right. You've seen one porcelain figurine, you've seen them all." Maggie furrowed her brow for a moment. "Charleston is stupid with haunted houses, cemeteries, and even haunted highways. Why not try ghost hunting? We couldn't get much more paranormal unless we were living in Transylvania."

"Darling, how are we going to find ghosts downtown? Where would they even sell EMF detectors like they use on the ghost hunting shows?"

"What can it hurt to try?" Maggie shrugged her shoulders. "Maybe we'll find a full body apparition in the municipal parking garage."

"Mom, the last time you went to a Halloween haunted house you peed your pants. If something unseen actually grabbed your ankle, you'd probably have an aneurysm."

"That kid totally caught me by surprise. Besides, they run haunted walking tours of the town for the tourists. It seems like a pretty tame jumping off point for novice paranormal investigators." Maggie pulled out a notepad and wrote *ghost hunting* next to number one on her list.

Cher scooped a generous spoonful of mayonnaise into the salad and did something she rarely ever did: spoke ill of her ex. "During my divorce proceedings, I went to the rifle range twice a week. Whenever I pictured Howard's lilywhite ass on the bullseye, my score improved dramatically."

"Are you suggesting that I add *shoot ex-husbands* to our list?"

"Mom! I absolutely forbid you to shoot Dad. He's a pretty good father and I don't have bail money."

"Target practice," Cher insisted. "We don't have to picture anyone on the target … unless we're feeling vindictive that day."

"I haven't fired a gun since I was a kid," Maggie said. "In those days, it didn't seem strange to drive to a gravel pit and hand a loaded .22 to your eleven year old. I don't imagine there are many parts of the country where it is still socially acceptable."

"You're standing in one, Mom. When I went to the state fair last summer I saw whole families, including infants, dressed in camouflage. South Carolina is hunting country, so wear your cammie baseball caps to the gun range and you'll fit right in."

"I'll add it to the list, Cher, but since this was your idea, you're not allowed to tease me when I shoot myself."

"It's human interest for my article."

After dinner and the consumption of many more glasses of cheap wine, the hobby list began to take a turn for the decidedly bizarre.

1. Ghost hunting
2. Target practice: rifles and handguns
3. Rock collecting
4. Photography - South Carolina wildlife
5. Soap making
6. Fencing
7. Belly dancing

8. Tie dying
9. Dog agility course training
10. Crawdad racing
11. Bull riding
12. Worm collecting

Despite the generous consumption of alcohol, raising sea monkeys never made it onto the list.

The dogs had finished counter surfing and were sleeping off a wiener orgy; Ted was fighting them for couch space while giving the TV remote a workout, waiting for the Sunday night game. Elena and George had claimed the leftover potato salad and headed back to George's apartment for what Maggie could only assume would be a night of gluttonous debauchery.

She and Cher were outside having a last cigarette before turning in. It was clearly understood that Cher would stay in the guest room anytime she drank at Maggie's house. She didn't seem to mind sharing the room with a drying rack covered in bras and sweaters, and it gave Fluffy a chance to snuggle up to his best friend on the couch all night.

"You know, darling, that Ghost Tours website looked pretty interesting. Maybe we should get tickets for tomorrow night before we sober up and realize how idiotic it is."

Maggie couldn't help but agree.

Chapter Six

It had been a long day in the lab. One of the interns had dropped a potshard on the floor, after having misfiled several buttons and a hair comb. Paul had laboriously glued the shard back together, while he sent the intern searching through the banks of drawers, looking for the missing items. Now he climbed the last flight of stairs to his fifth floor apartment hoping, as always, to build up some definition in his thighs and calves. He didn't have the time or patience for going to the gym, so the stairs were his one concession to fitness. As he rounded the last landing and stepped out into his hallway, he was brought up short. Why would Dr. Peters be waiting at his apartment door? He was sitting on the floor, back to the wall, so had apparently been there for some time. Paul was so wound up that he immediately assumed something had gone wrong. Had his advisor decided that Paul's find was not worthy of pursuing?

Dr. Peters shifted the paper bag on his lap and stood to his full six-foot height. He smiled at Paul. "Sorry if I seemed abrupt earlier. I had to prepare for a class, but I wanted to take a little time to celebrate your Wind Clan discovery properly."

Paul's knees nearly crumpled with relief. "That would be great Dr. Peters. Then I can show you the aerial photos of the settlement."

"Paul, when we're not on campus, you can just call me Sam. We'll be working together closely, and I'll probably join you in the field from time to time to inspect progress on the dig. Once you finish your thesis and get your doctorate, we'll be colleagues."

Paul wasn't sure he felt comfortable being on a first name basis, but he tried it out. "C'mon in, Sam," he said as he opened the door to his apartment. The building was new, but had been built to give a converted warehouse feeling, with a large open space and high ceilings. He paid his own way for most things, preferring to live off what you could laughably call a salary for working in the lab. His apartment took up one quarter of the fifth floor and was in a good section of town, at the insistence of his parents. Gene and Dora Lakeland didn't seem to take a personal interest in most areas of his life, but they were meticulous where his safety was concerned. They helped him financially to get this place, but it was he who kept up the payments and paid the bills. His brother Dan seemed to command their hearts, but sometimes Paul felt more like their asset than their child.

Paul had furnished the apartment himself, so he had little more than a couch, table with two chairs, and a bed. He was startled by the echo of Sam's voice off the raised ceiling. With just him and no television, the apartment was generally silent. His favorite part of the open space was his study. A large worktable littered with books, maps and photographs sat next to a row of bookshelves perfumed with the heady musk of old paper.

He was fascinated with the Native American lifestyle prior to and during the arrival of early European settlers. His computer was bookmarked with hundreds of sites recounting oral traditions of early Native American legends. His bookshelves were stocked with maps and stories of the early settlers' encounters with the indigenous population. He couldn't get enough of literature on the changing dynamics when two entirely different civilizations were thrown together. This was anthropology at its finest.

Sam was in his kitchenette, opening cupboards, looking for drinking glasses. He had pulled several two liter bottles of cola and a bottle of 151 proof rum out of the paper bag. "I thought we should celebrate your discovery in true scholarly fashion. Real scholars don't sit around with tea and scones in this day and age."

Paul rarely drank, so he was surprised at how smooth his rum and cola tasted.

"Here's to you, Paul. Your hard work has paid off."

Paul was a little embarrassed at the praise. "Here's to the Muskogee Indians. Their heritage lives on."

They went on to toast the University, the Supreme Court, and the mini-mart down the street. In the end they were toasting the Prime Minister of England and athlete's foot medication. At that point, Paul passed out and slumped over where he sat on the couch.

Sam eyed him carefully, poked his arm, and put down the cola without rum that he had drunk since the second round. He went to the worktable and studied the photographs. They were aerial shots of a large section of forest. What appeared to be trails cutting through the vegetation seemed somehow wrong. He squinted and saw the regular rectangular patterns. Centuries of exposure to the elements hadn't destroyed every trace of the town walls. There was no visible evidence other than mounds, but he could imagine the central square, which differentiated Creek towns from villages.

He proceeded to search the apartment methodically for any sign of the clay jar. Because of the sparse furnishing, it didn't take long before he conceded that the jar was not there. Paul must have taken him seriously when he was told to keep it under wraps. *Damn!*

He looked at his watch: still early enough to run to the office supply store and make copies of the photographs. Given time to study them, he might be able to get a better bead on the site's exact location. Sam had put enough rum in Paul's drinks to float a dump truck. There would be plenty of time to return the photos to the apartment. He borrowed Paul's briefcase to carry them and made his exit.

Everything seemed quiet. From his vantage point, parked across the street and a half block down, he had watched the blond man drive away ten minutes ago. Bear's hands felt clammy as he zipped up his leather jacket, crossed the street, and entered the building. There was nobody within sight to identify him. He wasn't sure even now if he could do it. How hard could it be? He had used his superior intellect to plan the perfect crime, but this spur of the moment opportunity was too good to be true. Sometimes the most elegant solution was the easiest. After all, most accidents happen in the home, and if the scene was set right, he could make this look like an accident.

It was a stroke of genius that Bear had chosen to follow the blond man after his meeting with Lakeland that morning. Since he already knew where Lakeland lived, he decided to trail this guy. The man had gone straight to the liquor store after leaving campus. When Bear saw the bag going into the apartment building with the man, but not coming out, he was reasonably sure that Lakeland had taken at least one drink with the fellow.

He checked the mailboxes in the lobby. Apartment 502, the fifth floor: that should be high enough to do the job. He had looked up how to pick a lock in the morning. You could learn anything on the internet. The motion of the elevator made him feel a little queasy. He swallowed back the bile in his throat, and with rubber-gloved hands, took hold of the knob; it twisted easily. The door swung open silently to reveal a large open space with the lights on and a man passed out on the couch. He saw the liquor bottle on the kitchen counter and took a deep sigh of relief. He couldn't have planned a murder any better if he'd tried. If his luck was this good, perhaps he should consider a new career as a contract killer. He grimaced at the thought. Even this necessity made him sick to his stomach.

It was a good thing he worked out regularly, because Lakeland's slack body felt like a bag of anvils. He thought of cartoon characters ... of anvils raining from the skies. How appropriate. He staggered out the balcony door and unceremoniously wrestled Lakeland over the rail. He leaned over to watch how his hapless victim's body hit the sidewalk below.

Unbelievable! He hadn't counted on the apartment's awning breaking the fall. Lakeland hit the awning on his side and rolled off what must have been the most sturdy canvas anywhere. After the final short drop, he lay limply on the ground, and then lifted his head, looking confused. It could only have been more of a cliché if Bear had done a double take. Who was this guy, a Hollywood stunt man?

Flummoxed, he began mumbling to himself, "The perfect crime. Hell. How? What now?"

He spun towards the door. Awareness hit him like a freight train. How could this happen? In his impulsive haste, he had forgotten to plan his exit. He must have been the worst super-villain ever! If this were the movies, there would be a fire escape at the end of the hall. He knew instinctively where he would find it, and that he would probably fall off the bottom landing and twist his ankle. It was one of those days.

Chapter Seven

"Hey, Donny! Saddle up, we got a jumper."

Jeanine Stout lived, ate, and slept next to her police band radio. She and her photographer, Donny, were eating a sumptuous dinner of take-out burritos in the back of the news van when the call came in. She took one last bite and jumped into the driver's seat for the short drive to the latest hot spot. She knew the streets of this community like the back of her hand. This was *her* beat, and she'd be damned if she let anyone get the scoop on her.

As she turned onto West 32nd, she could hear sirens in the distance. What incredible luck! She was first on the scene. She pulled up next to a pick-up near the corner and hit the pavement running. Nothing would get her kicked off the site faster than blocking the way for emergency vehicles.

Four people were gathered around a man lying on the curb. One woman was crouched down, touching his shoulder tentatively while talking to him. Donny outstripped Jeanine. He could run faster with a camera on his shoulder than most people could without. She did her best to catch her breath as she turned the microphone on.

She crouched next to the man and the other woman backed off. "I'm Jeanine Stout from News 2. What's your name?"

Paul gingerly touched his lower lip and looked at the blood on his finger. It was busted for sure.

"What?"

"What's your name, sir?"

"Oh, Paul. Ummm, did you see my glashes?" Paul slurred.

Jeanine spotted the glasses a few feet away and handed them to Paul. The frames were bent out of shape, but the lenses were intact. "Paul, did you jump off the building?"

Paul looked confused. "Was I s'posed to?"

"Have you been going through some rough times lately?"

In answer, Paul leaned over and threw up. There was no mistaking the reek of alcohol. Jeanine cringed as some of the vomit splashed on her pant leg.

A police car pulled up and an officer jogged their way, arms spread open. "C'mon folks. Let's back it up."

Only time for one more question: "Why did you jump, Paul?"

"Yur perty." Paul gave her a crooked smile as the policeman stepped between them.

"Okay Jeanine, you got your footage. You'll have to move back now."

Jeanine made a note to talk to Paul's neighbors for some background to the story as soon as the furor calmed down. More police were pulling up, and her priority right now was to stay close enough to listen in on the exchange between Paul and the police. She hadn't really expected to get anything coherent out of the jumper, but perhaps she could salvage a decent story out of it. Donny walked a few yards away and started taking background footage of the scene.

Sam Peters' palms were sweating. He seemed to catch every red light as he hurried back to Paul's apartment to return the "borrowed" photographs. He didn't count on it taking so long to fight the traffic and get the copies made. All the copiers but one were down, and the woman using it must have made one hundred copies of a page from a coloring book. He wondered how many boxes of crayons she would buy.

Police cars with sirens blaring passed him, going in the same direction. He slowed and pulled to the curb down the street from the front door. From there, he could see the crowd gathering around Paul, who sat at an awkward angle, his glasses askew. The police were crowded round him and trying to get him to lie down on the sidewalk. One woman was pointing upward while talking to the officer who appeared to be in charge. Sam got out of his car and strolled over to take his place at the back of the crowd of onlookers.

"So do you think he jumped, or did he fall?"

"I'm not sure, officer," the woman said. "I only saw him bouncing off the awning and falling to the ground."

The police talked among themselves. Sam could only imagine that they were weighing their options. How could he have known that Paul would regain consciousness before he returned? Had he gone out to the balcony for some fresh air, to clear his head? He staggered around badly enough now as he tried to stand, that he might have stumbled and pitched headfirst over the rail.

Sam felt a stab of guilt for his part in Paul's near-death experience. Fortunately, he was able to squash that emotion immediately. It was well known in the department that Paul could be clumsy. That certainly wasn't his fault.

"Sir, he's obviously hammered. Do we take him in for public intoxication, attempted suicide, or unlawfully good luck? This guy should play the lottery."

"He says he doesn't remember a thing. I don't think he jumped—probably fell. Call an ambulance so he can get checked out at the hospital. They'll have the psychiatrist talk to him to make sure he wasn't trying to hurt himself. It's a good thing he's drunk. If he hadn't been as limp as Gumby when he landed, he wouldn't be alive."

Sam caught movement out of the corner of his eye and turned his head. *Damn!* A cameraman was walking along the street, panning the crowd of onlookers. Sam retreated to his car to wait it out. Would the police check the apartment? His fingerprints were all over the bottle. It was pretty damning evidence. He was relieved when, after packing Paul to the hospital, the police left, apparently concluding that it was an accident. He waited for three-quarters of an hour before entering the building. He had no problem returning the photographs. Nothing looked different from when he'd left, other than the open patio door. If Paul had noticed the missing photographs while stumbling to the balcony, he wouldn't remember it in the morning.

What should he do now? The bad guys always wiped away fingerprints at the crime scene. It seemed like a compelling argument for cleaning up, but there was no denying that he had been there. Paul would remember that much. In the end, he wiped the counter and the bottle, but left his empty glass on the counter. No need to advertise that he had been the one pouring. He took one last sweeping look around the room before heading home.

Bear limped back to his truck, still parked down the street from the building. Could he call it, or what? The rungs on the fire escape had long ago rusted through, and his weight was more than the weakened steel could bear. The drop wasn't far, but he had landed awkwardly in a pile of plastic bags, which split open upon impact. He had the wind knocked out of him, and as he was finally able to suck in air, he realized how rancid it was. He counted at least four rats the size of terriers, and one of those refused to run away. It was unnerving to see the creature's black button eyes latched onto him, unflinching in the dark. He had felt something squirming under his hands, and shuddered at the thought of maggots making their way into his pants.

As he emerged from the alley into the street lights, he looked down at his pants. *Great!* There was a rip that went from knee to thigh, then continued up through his leather jacket. Apparently, his clothes had caught on a sharp edge of the broken ladder rung. There wasn't any blood on his leg, but he gave a shudder at the proximity of the tear to his manhood.

He hobbled around to the front of the building, and was alarmed to see one police car after another pulling up all along the street. Worse yet, a news van double parked next to his truck. As he backpedaled, ducking around the corner, he nearly bumped into a young couple, hurrying over to see what was going on. They grimaced, and veered off across the street, giving him a wide berth. He could hardly blame them.

The perfect crime. At least nobody had seen him enter the building, and they tried to politely avoid him as he left. As long as they didn't photograph his truck, he wasn't going to need an alibi for this fiasco.

He smelled like rotting cabbage, his ankle was killing him, and he was pretty sure that there was a piece of gum stuck in his hair. God only knew how long he would have to wait there before the news crew left. A woman walking by paused before him, pulled a dollar out of her purse and pressed it into his hand.

"God bless you, honey."

Paul came out of his blackout in the emergency room. Awareness hit him as he was mid-sentence, talking to the nurse. He had no idea what he had been saying, and wasn't even sure how he'd gotten there or why. He just knew that he ached in more places than not. The doctor said he was lucky to get away with only scrapes, bruises, and a broken pair of glasses. The last thing he remembered was having a drink with Sam. No, scratch that. He remembered having multiple drinks with Sam. *Geez, what a way to make an impression on your faculty advisor!* He silently prayed that he hadn't done or said anything embarrassing.

A policeman had followed the ambulance and was there to take his story. Unfortunately, all he remembered was throwing up on a pretty girl. *Oh my God! How on earth do you resurrect any dignity after that?*

"So before the fall, the last you remember was drinking with Sam Peters?" the officer asked. I'll get a statement from Dr. Peters to see if he remembers anything useful to help figure out how you ended up chewing asphalt."

What next, he wondered just as the psychiatrist came in. Paul tried to explain to the man that he was not depressed and had no thoughts of hurting himself.

The TV was playing softly in the background, and Paul's attention was caught by a familiar voice.

... live coverage...Have you been going through some rough times lately?

Paul looked up at the TV in time to see himself throwing up on the reporter. "Just kill me now!" he muttered.

"What was that, Mr. Lakeland?"

The psychiatrist's curious gaze unnerved him. One more word and they would lock him up and throw away the key. "Nothing, I was just ... nothing." *Nice save!*

Once the doctors pronounced him too ignorant of the laws of physics to have died, he was released and took a taxi back to his apartment, where he promptly passed out on the couch. The evening had come full circle.

Chapter Eight

Maggie and Cher sat at the kitchen table, drinking coffee and nursing headaches. Cher had not washed up or taken down her hair before going to bed. Her usual perfect French roll was dangling at an awkward angle, with long strands of loosened hair trailing around her face. The bags under her eyes were liberally smudged with mascara. Maggie hadn't looked in the mirror, and didn't even want to guess what she looked like.

"Where's that damn list?" Maggie grimaced as she rubbed her forehead. "If we don't get started on a hobby, my head will have exploded for nothing."

"I think we put it in the oven," Cher replied with a yawn. "Something about half-baked ideas."

Buddy started his morning yapping. He was determined to protect them from evil blueberry muffins.

He seemed to be saying that he would willingly throw himself on the offending pastry, rescuing them from the caloric grenade. Maggie and Cher cringed at the noise and quickly tendered a muffin to shut him up. Fluffy merely laid his massive head on Maggie's knee and drooled profusely. He received a muffin as a reward for not barking. It was a win-win situation for canine-kind.

Cher had to step over Buddy to retrieve their list from the oven. By now he had finished the muffin and was rolling in the crumbs, having little doggy orgasms.

Ted strolled into the kitchen in a t-shirt and pajama bottoms, looking way too chipper for present company. He snagged a muffin and poured a cup of coffee. "What are you girls up to today, and should I notify the authorities?"

"I'm planning to starch all your shorts before lunchtime," Maggie grumbled, adding, "Bwa-ha-ha!"

"I think that was specifically addressed in our marriage vows."

Cher looked over the list they had made. "Our first hobby is paranormal investigations," she mused. "Does that mean we have to stay up all night staking out some graveyard?"

Maggie grunted and propped her head up with one hand. She turned a bleary gaze up to Ted. "If we don't come out alive, there's a pot pie in the freezer."

He kissed the top of her head and whistled a cheery tune as he sauntered out with his coffee.

"I'm glad we're starting easy." Maggie slumped over, her arms crossed on the table, and her head resting on her arms. "The ghost tour will be good hands-on research before we fly solo. We can eat some dinner, then have a professional ghost guide show us the hot spots."

"I hope the tour provides us with the proper equipment. We should probably get some practice using phantom finders and spook speakers before we go off on our own. Let me know what time you want me to pick you up. I need to go home and run some laundry today. Do you think that my red dress would be appropriate attire?"

"Only if we're ghost hunting in the local bars, although that dress seems to attract some pretty spooky looking guys. Be sure to wear something that goes well with sneakers. Those cobblestone sidewalks can be hell in heels."

"I'll think of something, darling. Why don't I come by around five-thirty. We can go to Hyman's for dinner. I'm in the mood for their crispy fried flounder."

Maggie's wine-soaked stomach gave a lurch and she mentally measured the distance between her and the bathroom.

Buddy was asleep in a bed of muffin crumbs, his legs jerking spasmodically. He was instantly awake and on the alert once Cher stood up.

"C'mon you little mutt. Time to go home."

Buddy started the same jumping routine as when he had arrived.

In the wake of Cher's departure, the silence was deafening. Funny, Maggie was praying for peace and quiet five minutes ago. She drained her coffee and headed for the shower. The hot water should either revive her or drown her. Either way, the headache would be over.

Late that afternoon, Cher arrived in her robin's egg blue 1954 T-Bird. Maggie loved that car. The sleek design was very sexy, and the opera windows were just adorable. She was a little hesitant about what to expect from Cher's attire, considering she had chosen the sports car for their outing. She was relieved when Cher stepped out in jeans and a sweater. Maggie would be willing to bet that it was cashmere. She herself was wearing jeans and a Gamecocks sweatshirt. In this region you were pretty much either a

Clemson fan, or University of South Carolina—the other USC. Football season was underway, so Maggie hoped that no Clemson fans were on the tour.

She had bought tickets to the combination ghost and graveyard tour. There was also a tour which included some kind of dungeon, but that seemed like overkill. They decided to take the haunted road to Charleston to get in the ghost-hunting mood. Where Bacons Bridge Road ran past old plantations, stately oak trees lined the sides, interweaving overhanging branches. The effect was that of a dark tunnel, dripping with tendrils of Spanish moss. There were still some old slave shacks visible in the undergrowth, and many people claimed to have seen ghosts of slaves trying to escape through the surrounding swamps. Maggie felt a tingling along the back of her neck just thinking about it.

Cher tested the limits of her car's handling capabilities, flying through the curves and speeding down the straight stretches. They reveled in the exhilaration until, all too quickly, they entered the Charleston city limits. They parked in the municipal garage and walked to the restaurant.

"So which one of us do you think is going to run first?" Cher asked as they waited for a table. "I mean, *if* we see a ghost."

"I'll be paralyzed with fear and hoping not to soil myself."

"Sorry, darling, but that's not the best defense mechanism. It's not even fight or flight. You would be toast if you were in the Serengeti."

"I'm not built for speed, and I don't fight anything with fangs and claws. Besides, I heard that ghosts are like T-Rex: they can only see movement. While I'm invisible, you'll be a moving target."

They were seated and both ordered the crispy fried flounder. It was the specialty of the house and never disappointed.

Maggie pursed her lips. "If we get really involved in paranormal investigations, will we have to move on to dousing rods, crystals, and transcendental meditation?"

"No, darling, but we may have to take a field trip to Scotland to find the Loch Ness Monster."

"I hope she's easier to find than the Lizard Man." Maggie glanced up and noticed a man two tables over taking their picture with his phone. "Cher, paparazzi at nine o'clock."

"Is he cute?"

"Think aging gorilla with a bad toupee. I think there was a woman with him a moment ago. I'm guessing his wife just went to the bathroom."

Without looking his direction, Cher picked her nose.

Maggie looked over to see him recoil in horror and stare fixedly at his plate. "Mission accomplished, sweetie. And might I add, ewww!"

"Then our work here is done." Cher popped a hush puppy into her mouth.

They finished their dinner and waited with the rest of their tour group at the entrance to the Market Place. Within five minutes, a woman appeared carrying a battery-operated lantern, which was designed to look like an oil lamp. The lamplight cast an eerie shadow over her face, while her dress of bright red and purple paisley floated around her plump figure. Her skirt looked like it was made entirely of silk scarves, and she seemed to glide more than walk. Maggie judged her age to be in her mid-forties, but her brown hair was already liberally streaked with gunmetal gray.

"If she starts doing the dance of the seven veils, I'm out of here," Maggie whispered from the back of the group.

"You said you weren't built for speed."

"She's not a T-Rex, so freezing won't do any good. I think I'll have to try to outrun her and hope she trips over a veil."

Suddenly the woman's head swiveled toward Maggie, and she leveled a gaze that seemed to pierce right through her.

Damn!

Chapter Nine

Maggie and Cher both jumped at Madame Zarga's booming voice as she began her spiel. It sounded as if she was channeling Ethel Merman. Still, she attempted to evoke a sense of mystery in the swooping cadence of her speech. "Tonight we are going to take a journey into time and space. We will unlock the mysterious realms of the spirit world, travel into the past, and tempt the fates that wait just outside the cosmic portal."

Every ghost in Charleston was going to hear them coming from blocks away. They began walking along Church Street towards St. Philip's. Madame Zarga floated to the center of the west cemetery, leaving a trail of jasmine and orange blossom in her wake. Maggie was wondering if it was perfume or fabric softener as their guide pointed to a monument.

"Here lies Bishop William Andrew Guerry, murdered in his parish office in 1928. The Right Reverend Guerry is recorded as saying that he was looking forward to the day when the Episcopal Church has a black bishop. His strong stand for social reform earned him a fatal gunshot wound from Reverend J. H. Woodward, a white supremacist. The church is presently struggling with whether or not to take a progressive stand on homosexuality among the clergy and to permit same sex marriages. Bishop Guerry is said to haunt this cemetery. Perhaps he is singling out individuals who cannot embrace diversity." Madame Zarga seemed to be getting bored with her own canned narrative. She whirled around to face one of the men in the crowd. "As a sensitive I can see citizens of the spirit world. You, sir—I feel a presence next to you. Perhaps Bishop Guerry is displeased at your homophobia."

The gentleman scowled, and his face grew red. "I work in the fashion industry. What are the odds that I'm homophobic?"

Undeterred, Madame Zarga plowed on. "You, Ma'am, in one of your past lives, you were a parishioner of this church."

The woman looked stunned. "However did you know that? I moved here from Tokyo four years ago. I'm an atheist, so it only makes sense that in my past life I was an American Episcopalian."

Madame Zarga seemed to know when to cut her losses. "Moving on!" She led them to a shabby looking parking lot next to a bright yellow building. "This is Poogan's Porch restaurant, named for the current owners' dog, Poogan. You can see the headstone for their beloved pet here in the front garden."

"I think this tour is going to the dogs," Maggie whispered.

"This was the home of Zoe and Elizabeth St. Armand." Madame Zarga intoned. "A woman dressed in black can be seen looking out the second story window. She is believed to be Zoe. Despondent over the death of her sister in 1945, Zoe became depressed and isolated."

Maggie's thoughts started to drift.

"... moved away several years later."

Cher nudged her as she started to rock back and forth on her heels.

"... is said to haunt the upstairs ladies room."

Snap! "A bathroom ghost?"

Heads swiveled her way. Maggie didn't realize that she had said it out loud.

"Darling," Cher whispered. "we have *got* to come here for lunch!"

"And order eight or ten iced teas."

Madam Zarga continued, "… his wife went upstairs to use the bathroom, when she heard a furious pounding on the door. She opened the door to find herself staring at a woman in a long black dress. The next moment, she was gone. The wife fled from the restaurant and returned to her hotel, leaving her husband at the table, wondering where she went."

"What's next," Cher whispered as they began walking again, "a haunted hair salon, or a spectral service elevator?"

Madame Zarga scowled in her direction. They stopped outside the municipal parking garage.

"Oh, please don't tell me …" Maggie was bouncing on the balls of her feet, her hands clasped tightly together.

"The city unknowingly built the garage over top of a Quaker cemetery."

Maggie and Cher both started laughing.

"Cher, we're parked on Pilgrims!"

"We drove over the departed."

"Ladies, really!" Madame Zarga barked. "If you can't behave yourselves, I'll have to ask you to leave. These people suffered for their faith in life, and face daily indignity in death."

Maggie was tempted to try to say "daily indignity in death" three times fast, but she managed to squelch the urge.

As they marched on, they learned of Lavinia Fisher, the woman in white who was said to haunt the Unitarian Cemetery. "She was imprisoned from 1819 to 1829 and hung in her wedding dress, after luring passing wagon drivers to their death and burying them in her basement." Madame Zarga's voice took on a low and malevolent tone. "'I'll see you in hell!' She spat at the townspeople as they put the noose over her head. Even in death, she has enticed men from the cemetery path, mesmerized by her beauty."

"Typical!" Cher rolled her eyes.

"You, dear, in the back: there is a spirit following you who claims to be your mother."

Cher smiled. "My mother will be shocked to learn that she's dead." She turned to Maggie. "Should I plan a wake or a big memorial service? We can hire male strippers."

"I think she would have wanted it that way."

Madame Zarga cleared her throat. "Mock the spirits at your peril! Your disrespect has angered them. Beware, lest they follow you home and haunt you for the rest of your lives!"

Maggie whispered, "Cher, that would make it so much easier to go ghost hunting. I can just open my closet and, voila!"

"I hope my ghost doesn't make a specter-cle of himself when he shadows me home."

"Ouch! That's a bad one."

"Ladies! I'm afraid I'm going to have to ask you to leave. Your unbelief is disrupting the cosmic portal. We cannot hope to find the ghosts of Charleston if you insist on defaming the supernatural realm."

Maggie and Cher scurried away, red-faced with suppressed laughter.

Maggie couldn't contain herself any longer. "Ha-ha, how are we going to be paranormal investigators if we ke-heep disrupting the cosmic portal?"

"I'm sorry darling. Being kicked off a ghost tour must be a new low in my life. My mom may be a retired Vegas showgirl, but I should still check with her before I hire the male strippers."

"I wonder if Bishop Guerry would find embracing showgirls as a challenge to diversity," Maggie mused. "Hell, I'm just trying to picture him embracing showgirls."

"Do you want to stop for a drink before we head home, darling? They're the only spirits we're likely to see tonight."

"That depends. Are you going to pick your nose?"

"I think this time I'll talk about my rash."

Chapter Ten

Andy passed the meatball sub to Dan and kept the cheese-steak for himself. The sun was shining through the grimy front window, as dust motes scattered over the invoices littering the desk where they sat. Andy had six different garages scattered along interstate 378, and visited each station at least twice a month. He especially liked the garage in Lexington, just west of Columbia. This was his only business that did motorcycle repairs, and Dan Lakeland was the man who kept it going. Andy suspected that Dan delegated quite a bit of the office work so that he would have more time to tinker on the bikes. As long as the shop was turning a handsome profit, Andy didn't care if the station's mascot, Cooter, was running the office.

Cooter was Dan's six-year old bloodhound. He usually lay unconscious through the day, unless they were on the trail of small game. Then he could work himself up to a shambling, unhurried gait. He was lying on the office floor now, his nose and legs twitching with the subconscious ramblings of primal instincts. Andy felt a stab of jealousy. His dreams were usually filled with concerns for his employees, broken equipment, and family drama.

"Hey, Andy, how are Lureen and the kids? Is Jasper still begging you for a guitar?"

"Nah. Instead, he started askin' to take ballet lessons. I think he was kiddin', but I nearly had a heart attack. We went to the music store the same day and got a guitar."

"Ha! He's got your number, Andy."

Andy Hawkins had come from a poor family, and with only a high school education, a driving ambition, and a love for cars, he had built his little empire. He had a body shop, a transmission repair, a tire and lube shop, two general auto repair garages, and the bike shop. He also had his own junkyard, which he used for parts and scrap.

Even with his flaming red hair, he was the most even-tempered person that you'd ever want to meet. He never forgot his humble upbringing, and regularly did pro-bono work for those in need. He jealously guarded Sunday morning as family time to attend the local Baptist church with his wife of thirteen years, Lureen, and his sons, Jasper and Garnet. He attended church just outside of his hometown of McCormick, and protected the church bus from a life of dereliction. He was not averse to bending the rules to get what he wanted, but he was unwilling to hurt anybody in the process.

"How about those Gamecocks last Saturday," Andy eyes lit with animation. "They were smokin'!"

"They threw it away in the fourth quarter."

"But they made Tennessee earn it."

Dan rolled his eyes. "Tennessee was off their game. The Gamecocks looked like St. Mary's team: The Fighting Little Sisters of the Poor. That may not be a fair example though, because I hear the girls are kicking butt this year."

Dan looked at the grease under his fingernails as he chewed on his sub. While his brother was working on his doctorate, Dan had attended junior college before switching to a technical school to follow his real love. Whether he was repairing motorcycles or building custom bikes from the ground up, he looked forward to getting to the garage every day. On the weekends, he would often hunt or fish with his boss. Dan was tall and pure muscle from long hours hefting bike parts. When they brought Cooter along on their hunting trips, it could get mighty cramped in the duck blinds.

Dan had never considered marriage, but he had no lack of volunteers to keep his bed warm. He kept his wavy light brown hair just long enough so the girls could run their fingers through it. The skull tattoo on his biceps, the three-day growth of beard, and his line of work helped to maintain his bad boy image, although his eyes were the guileless bright blue of cornflowers on a sunny day. He was 28, but he preferred girls in their early twenties. They seemed to like the bad boy image.

Dan had been in far fewer barroom brawls than most of his coworkers, if that was any measure of a man's character. He thought it should count for something. He had a small apartment in Lexington, two Harleys, and a beat up pickup truck. His mom complained of the greasy state of his clothes when he stopped by to do his laundry, but she always made him stew with cornbread, or pot roast with mashed potatoes and gravy.

"We haven't been out boar hunting yet this season," Dan said. "Are you ditching me for some other guy?"

Andy laughed. "Maybe I should get my feelings hurt. You seemed to prefer the company of Sarah Howard last Saturday, as I recall."

"I took her to Ruby's, but it turns out, she didn't think that camouflage was appropriate for a first date."

"How does Sunday sound for you?" Andy asked. "We can pack up some gear and head out for some boar after church."

"I can roll with that. Just remember, I don't put out on the first date."

The men continued to size up the Gamecocks' chances for a winning season as they finished their sandwiches.

"My money is still on the Little Sisters of the Poor." Dan licked marinara sauce off his fingers, and offered the last bite of his sandwich to Cooter. The old hound was asleep again before he finished chewing.

Maggie decided to take the day off from hobbies. Cher had gone to the gun shop to have her two rifles and revolver cleaned today, leaving her with nothing to do but watch judge shows and catch up on laundry. If Cher finished early enough, perhaps they could "take tea" at the Victorian Tea House. It was a luxury that Maggie loved, but could seldom afford.

Before their first visit they had gone online to read the proper rules of etiquette, published by the Royal Family. They took care to fold the sugar into their tea, rolling the spoon exactly two to three times, rather than stirring it around. They were meticulous in the proper placement of their napkins if they had to get up to use the loo. Only once did Cher slosh her tea and drop a bite of scone on her lap. She left an extra big tip, to make up for her shocking lapse in decorum.

Maggie turned off the TV, and in the sudden silence, the ticking of the wall clock sounded deafening. A year had gone by since Maggie worked as a retirement fund administrator. She had endured continuing education webinars on changes to the Internal Revenue Code, and weekly department meetings. Sleepless nights had sent her head crashing to the desk at work on more than one occasion, and she routinely saw Excel spreadsheets scrolling before her when she closed her eyes. Now when she closed her eyes, she had only the darkness to keep her company. Sally was right, she needed a sense of purpose.

Maggie was folding Ted's shorts, which she hadn't starched, when Cher called.

"Bad news, darling, the doctor's taking next week off, so they want to squeeze me in today. I'm afraid we won't be able to do tea."

"There's nothing wrong, is there?"

"Just my annual pap smear. Believe me, I'd rather be sipping than stripping this afternoon."

"I'm envious."

"I'll tell you what. If you can hit the target tomorrow morning, I'll spring for tea to celebrate."

"I appreciate your faith in me."

"Just so we're clear, the target is that paper thing down the range. Shooting the tires out on my car is considered a foul."

"Your tires are safe with me."

"Oh, they just finished with the guns. Gotta run!"

Maggie heard the front door open as she hung up the phone. She tried to remember where she had put the baseball bat, when Ted sauntered in with a bouquet of flowers and a devilish grin.

"Just landed a big deal, so I thought I'd take the afternoon off to spend time with my favorite girl."

"Can I tag along?"

"You, my dear, are the main attraction."

He stroked her cheek as she stood up, the warmth trickling down her neck and tingling in her left breast. His fingers moved to her collarbone, where he began brushing gently along the base of her neck and across her shoulder.

"Ummm," she sighed as she rose up on her toes for a long, slow kiss. Ted kept up the light feathery strokes with maddening persistence. The tingling in her breast intensified and spread to her right breast, causing a heavy sensation. *Oh, God!* She wanted to bottle that feeling.

"Good thing I didn't starch your underwear," she said as they broke the kiss. "I wouldn't want to cramp your style."

Without another word, he threw her over his shoulder and galloped off toward the bedroom. She squealed, taken by surprise.

Damn! she thought. "I think I peed myself a little."

Ted threw her on the bed, and started doing things that made her immediately forget that little detail. She had to admit, this was way better than tea.

Chapter Eleven

Cher put on her reading glasses. "Good Lord, could they make the print on these Forest Service maps any smaller? The closest rifle range in the National Forest is named Boggy Head. We could try it out for our first attempt at target practice."

"Sounds scenic, in a swampy sort of way. I guess since we messed up the cosmic portal Monday night, we can't be too picky." Maggie examined the two rifles, and revolver on the kitchen table.

"That's not the worst. The range is right next to the Hellhole Wildlife Management Area. At least it's a beautiful day to go to hell."

The morning sun poured into Cher's bright kitchen as they drank their coffee.

"Is there ever a perfect day for firing small ordinance?"

Cher set two rifle cases on the table and packed up her .22 rifle and a .243. They were good beginner rifles: fairly straight shots, with little kickback. She also had an old .22 revolver, which held ten rounds.

"Is this the kind of gun they use to play Russian Roulette?" Maggie asked, eyeing the gun dubiously. "I thought revolvers had to be six-shooters."

"The ten-shooter gives you a little statistical edge in Russian Roulette. Still, it's not a game I would recommend, darling. The sudden death overtime is a killer."

Before they could pose a clear and present danger on the rifle range, they had to load up on ammunition. Maggie felt like she was having an out of body experience as she gazed at the boxes of bullets on Cher's counter. At least Boggy Head would be closer than they had gone for the Lizard Man expedition, which would give Maggie less time to consider the pros and cons of such an ill-advised adventure. "Sweetie, you know I trust you completely, but are you sure you have the right kind of bullets for these guns? I think they come in different sizes."

"Caliber, darling. Basically, the big bullets go in the big gun, and the little bullets ... you get the idea."

"So, when you had the guns cleaned yesterday, did they have a special place where you can wash them out?"

"They don't actually wash the guns. The process is similar to dropping off your laundry. Just be sure to keep your claim check."

With guns, bullets, and false optimism, they set off for the rifle range.

"Okay, darling. In South Carolina, the guns have to be packed properly and out of sight in the car in case we get pulled over."

"Well, if we get pulled over, "I'm letting you do all the talking. The minute I open my mouth, the cop will know that I'm a rookie. I'll probably get the one-hour lecture on gun safety. Speaking of which, you'll have to show me how to take the gun off safety once we're ready to fire."

"Don't worry, I'm wearing the low cut v-neck camouflage shirt so that the guys will help us if we get in a pinch." Cher smiled wickedly.

"I wish I had known. I would have worn my camouflage girdle. How much do you want to bet they actually make those?"

"Stealth underwear is no big deal, darling. I once saw a wedding dress made out of camouflage. I guess the punch line is: 'she bagged her man.' That leaves the door open to some pretty weird stuff on the wedding night."

Maggie made gagging noises. "Thank you for getting that visual stuck in my head."

So at 10:30 on a beautiful Wednesday morning, they pulled into the rifle range. It was about what Maggie expected, although she was a little disappointed that there was not a single tin can to be found. She had only managed to hit a can once as a kid, but it had made a very satisfying clanging noise. She would have liked to square off against her old nemesis as revenge for all the times she tried to lose weight eating nothing but soup.

The rifle range was little more than an open pit. There was a covered patio, with a row of semi-circular picnic-like benches. You could either stand at a firing position, or sit on the bench, your elbow on the hard wood of the table, propping up your rifle. Maggie had imagined earthwork foxhole wallows. She would have felt silly lying on her stomach, playing GI Joe. She was happy to leave the commando stuff to somebody else. To her surprise, most of the firing stations were occupied on a weekday morning. She guessed the age range of the men to be from old to older. The men appeared to be in their eighties, and several were sitting down with their rifle barrels propped up on a pillow. It didn't seem like a very practical way to go deer hunting.

"How do we set up the targets?"

Cher knew the drill. "We ask people to stop firing as we go downrange. Let's set up your target at fifteen yards, and I'll put mine at fifty yards."

They taped their targets to some cardboard boxes sitting next to the range, set them up at the appropriate distance, and weighted them down with large rocks.

Cher took up her position at station five. She showed Maggie how to load the .22 bullets in the rifle's magazine, as she loaded the .243. Satisfied that she had put the bullets in the proper hole and facing the right direction, Maggie cocked the bolt to chamber her first round.

"Is there some etiquette like in bowling? I guess I shouldn't fire a bullet at the same time as the guy in the lane next to mine."

"You definitely shouldn't fire a bullet *at* the guy in the lane next to you."

Maggie sat down, hoisted the .22, rested her elbow on the table, and took careful aim at the paper target with the man's silhouette. She lined up the sites on the barrel and squeezed the trigger, only to realize that the safety was still on.

"Rookie mistake," she muttered as she released the catch and aimed again. This time when she squeezed, an explosion thundered in her ear and rocked her backwards slightly. Once her heart slowed down, she peered at the target to see where the bullet hit. She had been trying for a headshot, but there was no bullet hole in the paper head. She scanned the rest of the body and saw nothing.

Cher looked through her scope. "Good job, darling! You got the target at station six right in the nuts."

"What?" Maggie shouted.

Cher handed her a set of earplugs, then stepped up and fired five shots in rapid succession. She landed two in the head, two in the heart, and one in the groin. Shooting obviously brought out her inner assassin.

"Remind me not to cut you off on the freeway," Maggie shouted.

"I see that there will be no stimulating conversation on the drive home. By the way, I've been meaning to mention that sweater. Orange is not a good look for you, darling."

"What?"

They took turns firing for another forty-five minutes before they stopped for a break. Maggie finally managed to hit her own target almost every time. She lowered her rifle and reached for a bottle of water. She realized too late that her finger was still on the trigger as she rolled the water around her gritty teeth. Suddenly, every eye on the range was focused on her as she stared stupidly at the crater in the concrete two centimeters away from her big toe. She felt a little dizzy as Cher carefully took the rifle from her and clicked on the safety.

"You should stick to your embroidery, Missy. This is no place for women," the man on her left said.

Maggie looked at her feet, feeling properly chastised, but Cher whirled around to the man at station six.

"What? Like you've never fired prematurely before?"

Maggie snorted, and the other men started laughing.

"I hear you've been firing blanks lately, Joe," the man at station four said.

"Ooh, too much information," Maggie giggled.

Cher emptied the guns and made sure that there was no live ammunition in the chamber. When they started discussing what to do with the leftover bullets, their range neighbors on both sides showed up. Apparently, surplus ammunition was much more exciting to their companions than Cher's camouflage décolletage. She took the slight with good humor.

"Do you want to come back?" Maggie asked simply.

"No. I think making loud noises is better appreciated by people with Adam's apples."

Maggie had worn her earplugs for the rest of the session, so her ears were no longer ringing. Now they just felt like they were stuffed with cotton. At least she'd made it through without having to make a visit to the emergency room.

"It's been less than a week and we've already crapped out on two hobbies. What's next on the list?" Maggie asked.

Cher pulled a notebook out of the back seat, while Maggie loaded the guns in the jeep. "I guess we better gather some gear and maps. Next is rock-collecting."

"Picking up rocks. That doesn't sound too hard. Is there a point to the exercise?"

"Well, I plan to carefully file away any pretty rocks we find on a shelf somewhere in the garage." Cher raised an eyebrow. "Seems like the only sensible thing to do with them."

"Before we start our collection, next is your birthday. You're turning fifty-three, if I remember correctly. Shall we go to dinner tomorrow?"

"You're good, darling. I can't even remember how old I am. Why don't you and Ted come over to my place for dinner?"

"You are *not* cooking your own birthday dinner!"

"You know that I enjoy cooking, and Jen will be there to help me. If you want to do something special, you could make your sinful carrot cake. No arguments. Dinner will be at six o'clock."

Maggie always made a point to observe special days with Cher, since her mother was the only family she had. Cher never knew her father, but she had put her mom up in a nice New York City apartment. Kitty Anderson had been a showgirl to pay the rent and keep food on the table. It had been an unusual upbringing, but they were as close as mother and daughter could be.

It was always hard to shop for a woman who could afford anything she wanted, so Maggie usually stuck with a card, a dessert, and flowers. Carrot cake was Cher's favorite, but she only made it for special occasions. Too much cream cheese icing and Maggie's belly button would be struggling to remain an innie.

Maggie dropped Cher at her home with the guns. She would bring Fluffy to the birthday dinner, so they could have another set of eyes staring at their dinner plates while they ate. It finally felt like her eardrums popped as she drove back home. She surreptitiously felt around to make sure her ears weren't bleeding.

Chapter Twelve

Thursday morning, Dr. Peters made a point of arriving early at his office. He parked his car in the faculty lot, and gathered his classroom notes. He had struggled through the evening to focus on preparing for today's lectures, but his mind was on fabled Indian burial grounds and lost cities.

The university upheld the tradition of publish or perish, but the unspoken question was, "What have you done for me lately?" The University of South Carolina's Archaeology and Anthropology Department was small and not nearly as well recognized as it deserved, but Sam had chosen it for its proximity to his first love: the birth of America. He loved everything about the early colonization period. There were pioneers, patriots, and pirates. The Carolinas were home to Edward Teach, the infamous Blackbeard. The child in him wished that he could spend a day on the rolling deck of a pirate ship.

The department head was always desperate to please the school administration, so professors were expected to regularly publish in the trade journals, gaining visibility for the school. The American Journal of Archaeology had just published an interesting story on establishing ethical guidelines for maritime archaeology, which often fell outside the government's jurisdiction. "Ethical." He tasted the word. With teaching, fieldwork, and writing, he was all about cutting corners, and ethics were little more than a nuisance when it came to getting the job done.

He had unearthed some amazing early settlements in the Charleston area, but things had been a little dry lately. He hadn't published a paper in over a year. If this wind clan discovery panned out, it was going to be huge. He was willing to bet that he could get a paper written before Paul could publish his dissertation. Paul had already done all the legwork; all he had to do was convince him to share his findings. Paul was a trusting sort, so it would be all too easy.

He could see a section of the student lot from his office window. Since Paul was normally the first one in to open the lab, Sam would know as soon as his car pulled up. The week was slipping away, and he had not been able to connect with Paul since that rum induced high dive on Monday.

Perhaps he still felt a twinge of guilt for having gotten Paul so drunk that he fell off his balcony, but in the end there was no real harm done. One way or the other, he needed to get another look at that jar before their excursion to McCormick on Saturday. Fortunately Mrs. Peters' little boy was gifted in the power of persuasion.

After trailing him for several days, Bear was surprised that Lakeland had not died in a fiery car crash long ago. The young man hardly needed his assistance to an early grave. The guy practically took corners on two wheels, he blew traffic lights, and he changed lanes like he was driving at Daytona. Bear knew that Lakeland was the first one on the campus every day, so his car would be alone in the student parking lot.

He arrived just before dawn, dressed in his hunting gear, ready to blend into the shadows if needed. Lakeland was already there, so he wasted no time scuttling toward the car, his small toolbox in hand.

Enough summer jobs working auto repair had given him a pretty good idea of which end of the wrench to hold. He marveled once again at how you could actually go online and find out how to cut brake lines.

Lakeland did a lot of driving around in the wilderness, so he had a Jeep Wrangler. Its high clearance allowed Bear to crawl underneath without any problems. He made tiny pinprick holes in both the front and back brake lines, and he disabled the dash warning lights. He would leave the emergency brake intact so the vandalism would not be obvious. As he bolted the chassis plate back into place, he heard a car approaching. Scrambling out from under the car, he dove for the nearby bushes. Bear had to stifle a yelp as he landed on a sprinkler head. James Bond wouldn't be lying here with a sprinkler up his ass and goose poop smeared on his knee.

The city of Columbia was rather flat. Using the emergency brake and shifting down would be enough for most people to stop. Mr. Speed Demon made gangster turns and frequently forgot to wear his seatbelt. There was no chance that he would be able to slow down in time once the fluid had leaked out.

As murders go, it was a bit sloppy, and there might be collateral damage to civilians. He regretted that possibility, but it had to look like an accident. He would catch the report on the nightly news. If he didn't have to witness the crash, he didn't expect to lose any sleep over the fallout.

By 8:00 AM, several interns had arrived to start the inevitable inventory of artifacts before classes. Paul's morning coffee was wearing off, so he decided to go get some breakfast. His favorite place was a bit of a haul from the campus, but the drive gave him time to clear his head before working on his thesis. Now that he had discovered the location of the Creek Indian town and burial grounds, he could start outlining his dissertation. The extensive research had paid off in spades.

The jeep handled strangely in the turns. He dreaded having to take time out to get it looked at, but he wanted it in good shape for the drive to McCormick on Saturday. He was still a little puzzled over his talk with Dr. Peters that morning. Sam kept coming up with reasons why he should examine the jar again before they left. All he had to do was ask. It seemed to Paul like an entirely reasonable request from a faculty member filing the necessary paperwork.

He was definitely off his game at the wheel, but he'd be better once he had his second cup of coffee. Just as he screamed up to a left hand turn, his tap on the brakes did nothing. He was going at an angle across the intersection. In the split second when he jumped the curb and rocketed towards a warehouse, he managed to pull the emergency brake. The car lurched but did not slow down significantly. As he approached the open warehouse door, he shifted down, still pressing his foot uselessly on the brake pedal.

Suddenly, he was hyperaware of everything around him. Time slowed down to a crawl. The sign over the door read, "Fowl Tendencies Bird Processors." He realized too late that he had not buckled his seat belt. Paul heard tires squeal, and smelled the overheated rubber on the concrete as the emergency brake took hold. As he crossed the threshold of the huge sliding doors, the change from light to relative darkness blinded him. He could only make out a big white blob in front of him.

As the jeep broke through a wall of hanging plastic strips, it veered to the right, throwing him out the half side door. His body didn't have enough time to stiffen up before he disappeared into a cloud of white. He was waiting to feel the crushing impact, which never seemed to come. Each millisecond passed with frustrating slowness, as the whiteness consumed him.

He was suffocating. He was swimming against a sea of fluff, which filled his nose and open mouth. He didn't know which way was up. He could hear muffled noises; maybe people were shouting far away. He felt something clutch at his shirt. Then something pulled at his arm. He emerged from the fluff, choking and spluttering. With each cough, he could see a spray of willowy feathers explode from his mouth and gently drift downward. He could understand snatches of conversations.

"Good Lord, boy ..."

"... miracle that you didn't ..."

"You coulda kilt somebody!"

The room was getting dimmer and his last conscious thoughts were that he should have worn his seat belt, and he never got his coffee.

"We're on the scene now at the Fowl Tendencies Bird Processing plant, where a man has just crashed his car into the warehouse. It is unknown at this time whether or not there are any injuries as a result." Jeanine turned to glance at the warehouse entrance.

Emergency personnel had already arrived before she got to the scene. They were just loading Paul into the ambulance.

"Unbelievable! Are you getting this, Donny? It looks like our jumper from Monday night."

This morning she had competition. Channel 7's crew had just arrived on the scene. She saw that John had broken away from the other officers and was walking toward his car. Sal Whitehead from Channel 7 was already making his way to John, so she jogged to catch up.

John looked up and saw them coming. He knew there was no way to get out of the confrontation. He had already been cleared by the department to give the basic facts to the press.

"John, what can you tell us about the accident?" Sal poked his microphone right under John's nose.

"Green 2005 Jeep Wrangler jumped the curb and drove into the factory. Drove through the loading area, spun out in the feather room. Driver was thrown from the jeep into a pile of feathers. The EMTs couldn't find any serious injuries on the driver and nobody in the warehouse was injured. The driver is conscious but groggy. They're taking him to the hospital for observation. Looks like he got really lucky. We can't release the name, and the cause is under investigation. They'll clear the area for you as soon as the car is hauled off."

Jeanine shoved her way past Sal. "The fellow over there talking to the officers, he witnessed the crash?"

"Yeah. You can interview him once he's finished his statement."

"Thanks, John." Jeanine gave him a wink. "I'll let you get to your paperwork."

John just rolled his eyes.

As she turned away, Jeanine had a small, satisfied smile. She didn't have to share the guy's identity with Sal. She still wondered if Lakeland had been trying to commit suicide. Two accidents in four days was just too weird to be coincidence. This was starting to present itself as a nice little mystery. She would have to talk to her director, but she was pretty sure he'd let her look into Lakeland's background a little further. She would definitely keep her eye on him over the next few days.

"Wow!" Sal said. "Crashing into a pillow factory. That must be the luckiest son of a bitch alive."

"You have no idea."

Chapter Thirteen

Maggie, Ted, and Elena arrived at Cher's house a half hour before dinner. George had been delayed at work when a shipment of alfalfa sprouts had been mistakenly advertised as a sale on Cheez Whiz spread. Ted went straight for the television, while Maggie and Elena headed for the kitchen to see if they could get in the way. Finding the kitchen nearly required a GPS and road signs.

Jen was helping Cher make lasagna when Maggie and Elena walked in. Buddy and Fluffy had both wasted no time getting themselves underfoot, begging for scraps of mozzarella cheese. Maggie laid the birthday card and carrot cake on the counter. She searched for a vase to hold her grocery store flower bouquet.

Cher blocked her way to the cupboard and held her ricotta cheese coated hands out to give Maggie an air kiss.

Unfortunately, Fluffy took that as an invitation to lick cheese off her fingers. She laughed, gave an air kiss to Elena, and bent down to offer the other hand to Buddy.

"Happy birthday, sweetie!" Maggie chimed as she searched for the vase.

"It is now. Glad you all could make it."

"Are you crazy? You'd have to change the locks to get rid of us. Hi, Jen. Has this old lady started getting crotchety yet?"

"No, but she's threatening to get out her crochet doily collection, and I caught her nipping at the brandy. I'm not buying the story that it's for her rheumatism."

Jennifer McNutt was the undisputed master of this domain. She had been Cher's housekeeper for nearly twelve years. Jen had married young, divorced young, and had no children of her own. At thirty-seven, she might hear her biological clock ticking, but she gave no indication of it. She was five foot six inches of girl next door, with the delicate build that Maggie could never hope to attain. She lived with Cher, in a mutually comfortable arrangement. Her sassy mouth, honesty, and good nature complemented Cher's personality.

"George sent over some tabouleh," Elena said as she set a bowl on the counter.

"That's a whole grain salad, isn't it?" Without waiting for an answer, Jen walked over to the refrigerator and started rummaging around on the shelf. "Bacon bits," she murmured. "Maybe that will make this crap edible."

Elena laughed. "George is still trying to push free samples of tofu at the store. He hasn't figured out yet that all they have to do is offer a sale on collard greens and fatback pork, and they'll have customers coming out of the woodwork."

Cher rinsed off her hands and got some wine glasses out.

"Can I help you with anything?" Elena asked Jen.

"That's all right, dear," Jen answered. "I think we've got everything under control."

Maggie and Elena poured themselves some Chenin Blanc while Cher put the flowers in a vase.

"Would you be okay to finish up here, Jen?" Cher asked.

"Only if it means you'll get out of my way. You guys are cramping my style."

Maggie pulled a bottle of beer from the refrigerator for Ted, and they trooped off to the living room.

The first time Maggie visited, she literally got lost in the 3,000 square foot home. The realtor had advertised it as a "starter estate." It was like having a mansion with training wheels. The house only had three bedrooms and three and a half baths, but they were palatial. Everything was a feast for the eyes. Cher even had marble flooring in her utility room. One of the study walls was lined with floor to ceiling bookshelves. Cher's tastes ran mainly to mystery and romance. Scattered here and there were classical literature and science fiction. Cher was not a book snob. You would find no leather bound first editions in her collection. Well-thumbed paperbacks and several sets of hard back series made up the majority of the library. Some inspirational books, several Bibles, and a few hymnals rounded out the collection.

One of the centerpieces in the house was a Steinway baby grand piano. Cher enjoyed pounding out her favorite songs and hymns. Her talents were passable. Maggie would sometimes bring her guitar and they would hold a mini jam session, singing old Beatles tunes. Neither of them was immune to the occasional sour notes and clinkers, but Maggie had a rich alto voice, which complemented Cher's soprano beautifully.

Maggie loved the mahogany claw-foot table in the dining room, and the chandelier in the foyer. The home was furnished with care by one of the best interior decorators in the Low Country. The only items that didn't seem to fit in were an overstuffed sofa, a dog bed, and a basket of toys in the great room. Even though Buddy didn't shed much, he was only allowed on his own couch. As it happened, this was the most popular piece of furniture in the whole house. It served as his entertainment center for all his adoring guests, both human and canine. It was where he and Cher snuggled to watch the news, judge shows, and old movies.

Ted was on Buddy's couch now, with dogs sprawled on either side of him. The evening news was just starting.

Bear waited anxiously for the news. They had run the story at the very end of the show as a public interest hook. It certainly was one of the most bizarre stories all week.

... Apparently, the brakes failed on his 2005 Jeep Wrangler. In an incomprehensible twist of fate, the rampaging rover careened into the Fowl Tendencies Bird Processors: a company, which, among other things, provides down feathers to the makers of comforters and pillows. The jeep and Mr. Lakeland came to rest in a room full of feathers going through their year-long drying process. He was taken to the hospital for observation, then released with only bumps and bruises. The doctors reported that Mr. Lakeland was egg-ceptionally lucky. This is Jeanine Stout for News 2 on the street.

He still had grease under his fingernails, a crick in his neck, and a man who absolutely refused to die. Bear was starting to believe in divine intervention. How in hell was he going to get rid of this guy before he blew the whole deal? Bear had worked too hard to let this opportunity slip through his fingers.

The accidental death scenario wasn't getting him anywhere. Time to take the more direct route: a simple inelegant gunshot to the head, which he could pin on somebody else.

As Ted changed the channel, Cher furrowed her brow. "Go back to the news, please. That feather guy … he looks familiar. I just can't remember where I've seen him."

"His facial features are a little like Howard's. He doesn't have any illegitimate children out there, does he?" Maggie asked.

Cher choked on her wine, and Maggie quickly patted her on the back. "Sorry, Cher, that was a stupid thing to say."

Cher's eyes were glistening. "Well," she quickly dashed the back of her hand over her eyes. "I'll just go see if Jen needs help with the salad."

Elena scowled at Maggie. "Really, Mom?"

"Looks like I need more wine," Maggie made her way to the kitchen, where Cher was slicing onions. "Are you all right, Cher?"

Cher sniffled. "Of course, darling. I seem to have gotten some really strong onions."

Maggie decided it was better to let it go. "I'm sorry that we haven't stuck with a hobby long enough to get you any research for an article."

"I think our problem has been not committing fully to a hobby; that and the fact that the first two ideas were pretty stupid."

"Those were the cream of the crop," Maggie said. "It all goes downhill from here. Even so, once I got home after nearly amputating my toe on Tuesday, I ordered a geological survey map and rock hammer. Next on the list is rock collecting, and we're going all out. Let's take a weekend and go somewhere with diamonds."

"I don't think we have time to go to South Africa, darling."

Maggie continued, undeterred. "I also got a book that lists different possible rockhounding field trips in the area. It has a list of the equipment and supplies we'll need. If we don't start right away, it'll be too cold to go out and we'll have to wait until spring. The map and pick will get here tomorrow, so we can head out tomorrow night or Saturday."

"We don't even know where we're going yet."

"We'll figure that all out when we get the maps. You know you want to do it, Cher."

"I just remembered. I have a lobotomy appointment tomorrow. What a shame that I won't be able to come with you!"

"No excuses. You can get your brain surgery anytime, but how often do you get a chance to dig up dirty old rocks?"

"Way to sell it, Maggs!"

Chapter Fourteen

Friday morning found Maggie poring over the geological survey map while Cher read aloud from *Exploring the Geology of the Carolinas*.

"No offense, darling, but isn't this a lot of trouble just to pick up rocks?"

Maggie was intent on her map. "What? Oh, this is research. This time we'll be prepared. We're on this big gray blob. Let's see ..." She examined the map's key. "... phosphate. I don't suppose that's code for emeralds. There's got to be something else nearby."

Cher continued to read. The state was divided into two halves. They lived in the low country—the area that made up the coastal plain, continuing along a large portion of the Eastern Seaboard. Bisecting the state was an area known as the fall zone. Early settlers could carry their goods upstream until the elevation change. Here, waterfalls blocked river traffic and necessitated portage of goods to the higher elevation. Many of the modern-day large cities along the Appalachians were built in the fall zone.

The upper portion of the state lay on the Piedmont, a mountain range at the time of ancient Pangea, which would become the lower Appalachians after continental drift.

Maggie looked at the map in dismay. Clearly, the low country was not a hot bed of geological wonders. The majority of the area was composed of clay and silt. She supposed that it should not have been a great surprise after trying to find any arable land in her flower garden.

"These yellow boxes with the x through them are sand. Downtown Charleston is on this pink blob. That's peat."

Cher looked up from her reading. "You mean that Charleston is built on a peat bog? How is it not sinking into the mud?"

"They probably filled it in with phosphate before building the city."

Along with the map, Maggie had ordered a box of rocks so they could compare and identify whatever they found. It was intended for school science projects. The clear plastic box had twenty-four compartments filled with the most common rocks and minerals in South Carolina. You couldn't get much more common than kaolin and fuller's earth. Most of the rocks had only commercial uses—the making of bricks and mortar was at the top of the list.

Marked in red along the fall zone were several deposits of gold, which had been mined in the early 1800's. Since Maggie didn't want to travel farther upstate to look for gems, she decided that the fall zone would be the closest area of interest.

"Look at this, Cher. The town of McCormick was built right over the top of the Dorn gold mine."

"Damn, and I forgot to bring my hard hat. I guess we'll just have to take a pass on entering a musty, crumbling mine."

Maggie looked up from her map. "You never know. It might be a damp crumbling mine."

"Where do I sign?"

While Maggie compared her geological map to her road map of South Carolina, Cher went over the book's list to look up supplies they would need. The list was much longer than she had expected, but most of it consisted of household items.

Cher looked up from her list. "You're sure we won't be thrown into some small town jail for claim jumping? I look really bad in orange."

"According to the *Earth Treasures* book, you can dig and pan in any wildlife management area in the National Forest … as long as you don't use automated equipment. McCormick is right in the middle of the Sumter National Forest so we should be okay."

"We don't have automated equipment. We don't even have gold pans, and I don't think that we're going to find any at the local hardware store. If you have your heart set on heading out this afternoon, we'll have to improvise."

Maggie went to the kitchen cabinets and started pulling out pots and pans. "We have an old tin pie pan, a Spanish paella pan and a wok. The paella pan and wok have handles, so they would probably be easiest."

"Do you have some rubber gloves, darling? That water is going to be cold, and I just had my nails done."

They gathered garden trowels, safety goggles, sandwich bags, markers, a magnifying glass, and their new rock hammer; they found an empty rusted-out toolbox in the garage and loaded their gear inside.

"Do you have flashlights, darling?"

Maggie pulled some flashlights out from one of her cupboards. She went through four of them before she found one with fresh batteries. "Better add batteries to our shopping list!"

At the last minute, Maggie remembered to throw in two pairs of rubber gloves and put the pans in the duffle bag with her clothes. They were only going for the weekend, so they packed light. Of course, they had completely different opinions on what constituted "light."

They loaded the toolbox, duffle bag, a bag of dog food, and Cher's suitcase and garment bag in the back of Maggie's jeep. The dogs leapt joyfully onto the backseat, and they were on the road by noon. Fluffy and Buddy were asleep by 12:05. They decided that for the mine, they would need lantern style flashlights. After a quick stop at the hardware store, and a fast food place they were heading for Columbia.

Cher slurped the last of her milkshake. "Are you sure that three days will be enough time to find our rocks?"

"We'll be walking around on top of a gold mine. How hard could it be? In fact, this map has *three* black dots with yellow blobs in the middle all around McCormick. I'm sure that somebody there can tell us how to find at least one of the mine entrances. We'll get an early start at the mine tomorrow, that way we should be done by lunchtime."

"As long as you don't spend the rest of the day dragging me to antique shops, Maggie. I'll never understand your fascination with old stuff."

Cher only used Maggie's given name when she was all business. Hopes of finding a vintage soap collection were fading fast.

At Columbia, they turned west onto highway 378. The road soon turned into a two lane highway and wound its way through the countryside, occasionally passing through one small town or another. Eight miles out from McCormick, they crossed a bridge over Hard Labor Creek. Maggie immediately pulled the car over and jumped out.

"Wait a minute, darling. What did you have in mind?"

"They obviously did some panning for gold in this creek. That would be how it got its name. I think we should do a practice run on the panning."

Before Cher could voice her objection, the dogs were out of the car and running down the bank to the water's edge. She reluctantly slid out of the car, took the wok from Maggie and trudged down after the dogs. Maggie followed with her paella pan and the toolbox.

Cher's navy blue slacks and printed silk blouse were better suited for lunch at the country club than panning for gold. She made a concession by wearing sneakers down to the creek, but her heels would be back on as soon as they returned to the car.

Cher looked at Maggie. "Why do we need the toolbox?"

"We'll want to bag up any gold we collect and note where we found it."

The stream was fast moving and filled with treacherous looking boulders. They wandered up and down the bank looking for a relatively sandy and calm stretch. Fluffy cavorted with Buddy at the water's edge, then came to stand next to Maggie before vigorously shaking. Somehow, neither of the dogs had felt the need to shake themselves near Cher.

As Maggie cringed and scowled at the sopping dog, her leather sole connected with a particularly slippery rock. The spindly tree trunk which she managed to grab slowed down her fall, but did not prevent her from smacking her shoulder against the crumbling bank and landing on her seat in a small sandy pool of water. Buddy wasted no time in splashing circles around her, and Fluffy happily sat next to her, squishing his butt back and forth to make a depression in the soft sand.

Cher had been observing Maggie's technique from the creek's bank. "I thought that just the pan was supposed to go into the water. I'm afraid I didn't dress for the occasion if it's a pool party."

Maggie snarled under her breath and planted her hands on the bottom to leverage her backside out of the sand. Her fingers sank through the sand to find something decidedly slimy underneath: a thick layer of mud. Standing up was no simple matter. She had to perform a rocking motion to work herself loose from the suction, before she was finally able to clamor to her feet.

"Did I get any on me?" She was wet and muddy from the middle of her back down to her heels.

"I would never have noticed if you hadn't said something."

"Well, between all the vegetation and dead critters that were decomposing in that goo, I should add a certain ambiance to the wet dog smell that we'll have in the car."

Cher sniffed in her direction. "An intoxicating bouquet, with just a hint of earthworm."

Maggie found some solid footing and they started up the bank to the car. She always kept a towel under the seat for Fluffy, but today it would have to do triple duty. After wiping down both dogs, she threw the towel over her seat and got in. They drove straight to their motel on the other side of town, barely taking in the quaint village feel of the town center.

They chose a motel based on the availability of rooms that allowed pets. Maggie glanced around the lobby as she checked in. There was a large plastic dispenser on the counter, with corn flakes on one side and raisin bran on the other. A crusty looking coffee machine with a chipped carafe stood next to it. She supposed that they would spice up the continental breakfast with some stale bagels and overripe bananas tomorrow morning.

She took the key card for 107 and parked the car in front. As they entered the room she was struck by the smell of stale cheese. "Ugh! What died in here?" Maggie asked.

"Don't worry, darling, I brought my secret weapon."

Cher pulled a bottle of Chanel from her bag and spritzed the bathroom. While Cher hung her garment bag, removed her fluffy bathrobe and slippers and set up her cosmetics next to the sink, Maggie changed out of her wet things, rinsed out her jeans and panties, and hung them over the shower rod to dry. She rinsed off in the shower, trying not to touch the walls or shower curtain and pulled out the only other pair of jeans that currently fit her. She didn't want to buy any more size eights, when she knew with a certainty that she would soon be back into a size six. Well, maybe just reasonably sure. They weren't likely to go anyplace fancy for dinner, so she should be dressed well enough.

Cher had changed into a sweater dress with a whimsical charm necklace, dangling with Native American depictions of animals. She touched up her lipstick, then let down and shook out her hair. She looked out of place with the threadbare rug and floral comforters, yet she seemed perfectly at ease.

"I hope the town has a decent restaurant." Maggie said. "Looks like the kind of place that rolls up the streets for the night at six o'clock."

"I love small towns. I often wondered what it would feel like to live in such an intimate setting. I suppose if the Mayor passes gas, it would be front page news."

"What a romantic thought. As long as it's not a Stepford community, we should be all right."

Even dressed to the nines, Cher could slip easily between cosmopolitan socialite and her humble Vegas upbringing. The life of a showgirl isn't all it's cracked up to be. The pay was barely enough to support a single parent and child, but Ruth worked hard to give Cher a normal and happy childhood.

They settled the dogs and headed out for dinner. Maggie might have rethought her wardrobe if she'd known what dinner would hold.

Chapter Fifteen

Jonathan Miller, Esquire sat at a corner table in the McCormick Inn, reading a legal brief from the Plaintiff's attorney. The civil case had come back in several mutations to plague his client, but they had avoided legal exposure each time. He was good, but he wasn't cheap, so multiple attempts at lawsuits merely meant more trips to his cottage on Martha's Vineyard.

Along with intelligence and ruthlessness in the courtroom, Jonathan was blessed with the stunning good looks of a movie star. He stood 6'1" of pure sculpted muscle. He had a large clientele of wealthy widows and divorcees ranging in age from their fifties to sixties. He wasn't averse to providing other services for them. He glanced at his Rolex watch, a gift from an especially appreciative woman.

His primary business office was in Columbia, but he still kept the small office and upstairs apartment on Main Street where he had started his practice. It came in handy for those times when he wanted to come home for the weekends. Home … ten years in the city and he still considered this dump his home. *You can take the boy out of the country, but you can't take the country out of the boy.* He would probably be up late this evening revising the brief, but tomorrow he planned on getting in some fishing.

Jonathan had been married to a plain and sensible girl. Ellen was from a good family who had paid his tuition for law school. Shortly after he passed the bar, his wife had been killed in a home invasion and robbery attempt, leaving her share of the family fortune to him. The identity of the thief was never determined. In grief, he had sworn never to marry again. Now at 33, he had kept his word, but he had no small number of one-nighters. He was always discreet about who he took to his bed.

As the inn's door opened, he looked up from his reading and his breath caught in his throat. There was an attractive woman in the doorway standing next to a goddess. He wasn't sure of their ages, but would guess that they were in their mid to late 40's. He took in the hint of Chanel and the Jimmy Choo pumps and handbag, but he had trouble taking his eyes off that sweater dress, which showed every artful curve.

The waiter seated them at the empty table next to his, and Jonathan unconsciously ran a hand through his wavy black hair. He tried hard not to stare, unlike the other men in the dining room. He couldn't help himself. As the women were discussing the specials of the day he spoke up. "I know that it's a terrible small town cliché, but they really do make a very good meatloaf. It's what I had. Are you ladies just passing through, or are you visiting somebody in town? My name is Jonathan, by the way."

"I'm pleased to meet you. My name is Maggie and this is my friend, Cher. We're on a mission. Do you know where we can find one of the gold mines around here? We want to do a little prospecting."

He was taken aback. "Just like that? It could take awhile to find anything."

Cher jumped in, "Please, if you could point us in the right direction, we can at least have a go at it. I'd like to write an article about our adventure, but there's no point if we can't even find a gold mine. I understand the town is built on a mine, but I haven't seen any signs pointing to the entrance."

Jonathan honestly didn't know where to begin. "You're a writer? You're looking for gold as an adventure? The mine entrance is down the street, but you can't dig there. They just offer tours, and I believe it's closed down for the season."

"There are other mines indicated on my map, but the detail isn't great." Maggie said. "I don't suppose there are any mines with historical markers or road signs pointing to their position? I just want to use my rock hammer on something before I leave. We don't have a lot of rocks in the Charleston area."

"I've lived here all my life, but I haven't gone hunting for gold since I was a kid. The area was covered pretty thoroughly during the rush."

Maggie scrunched her eyes in thought. "Maybe you could tell us where we can find National Forest land that isn't leased out to the lumber companies or privately owned. There were *no trespassing* signs just about everywhere we looked driving in here."

"I'd recommend going into Sumter National Forest north of town. There are many Wildlife Management Areas that are open to the public. You'll just need to be careful, since deer hunting season opened last week. Be sure to wear bright colors if you're going into the woods."

"Thank you. That's excellent advice," Maggie said.

He opened his briefcase to put away the legal papers and pulled out a business card. *Leave them wanting more,* he thought. "Here's my card. Maggie, Cher, if you ladies need anything while you're in town, please don't hesitate to call."

Cher actually batted her eyes. "You've been a great help already. Thank you so much."

Playing it cool with the ladies had been no trouble in the past, but now, as he tried to make his grand exit, he stumbled and knocked into their table. With a quick apology, he turned for the door. Cher's eyes followed Jonathan as he stepped out into the evening light.

"Are you just going to watch him ride off into the sunset?" Maggie asked as the waiter approached.

"Do you know what you'd like?" he asked.

Cher continued to stare stupidly at the door.

"Yes," she breathed.

"Sweetie, he means for dinner."

Saturday morning found Dr. Peters waiting at the curb in front of Paul's apartment building.

"Thanks for driving today, Sam. They said that it would take about a week to complete the repairs to my jeep."

"You're damn lucky to have walked away from that with only some bumps, and bruises, and feathers up your ass. If I didn't know better, I'd say that someone has it in for you."

"What can I say? I live a charmed life, but if I have another accident, my insurance company will probably put a bounty on my head." Paul chuckled as he loaded his camping gear into Sam's SUV. "I'd say I'm having some bad karma if it weren't for discovering the burial site."

"I have two words for you, Lord Carnarvon."

Paul laughed. "Oooh, the mummy's curse."

Sam could barely keep a straight face as he said, "He died within one year of discovering King Tut's tomb. I'm just saying, Paul."

"I never imagined that archaeology could be such a dangerous job when I signed on. I'll sleep with one eye open tonight."

Talk naturally turned to the burial site.

"Initially, we'll have to date the jar according to other pieces in the archives," Paul said. "I've already begun gathering confirmed pieces from that time period. We'll need to check for similar clay composition, glaze patterns, and density. We should be able to start a detailed examination within the next two weeks."

"What about the native town ruins you found nearby?"

"I haven't had a chance to really examine them other than the aerial photographs. I'm anxious to get an initial trench started as soon as possible. "

"You know, Paul, if this is the Wind Clan, I think we can get *National Geographic* in on it. They have wet dreams about this shit."

"I know it's going to be pretty hard to prove, but if there are more artifacts at the site as definitive as that jar, we stand a good chance."

"*You* stand a good chance, Paul. I'm just here to make sure you dot the 'i's and cross the 't's. This is your find."

Paul was just naïve enough to believe him.

Chapter Sixteen

The sky was a brilliant blue on Saturday morning, with a chill in the air. In South Carolina it meant sweater weather, so if they went panning, the water would feel icy. Maggie went to the motel office to pick up some coffee for her and Cher. Yep, she had called it. Next to the cereal dispenser was a bunch of overripe bananas and a paper plate with dried out bagels. The coffee looked and smelled like hot tar, as if it had been sitting all night. Apparently, nobody else had felt inclined to drink it, since it was still untouched in the pot. Deciding to pass on the continental breakfast, she and Cher went down the highway to a small Mom and Pop diner. The moment they stepped out of the car they could feel the bacon grease seeping into their pores, the tantalizing aroma made Maggie's mouth water. The food was cheap and the coffee was like heaven. It was classic southern cooking.

They burned through several cups of coffee and a couple cigarettes during breakfast.

Cher snuffed her cigarette. "Have we decided where we're going today, darling? Maybe we should try up north like Mr. Hunkalicious suggested. I swear, I slept with his business card under my pillow last night."

"In school we used to say that if you dream about a guy, you're going to marry him. So, were there any naughty nocturnal thoughts?" Maggie asked.

"No, but I dreamt my gardener told me that I had killed my azaleas."

"Don't worry, sweetie, I'm sure they had it coming. Yeah, I think it's best to head north like Mr. Miller said. Do you have your bright yellow cashmere sweater? We wouldn't want to be mistaken for deer, or tourists."

"Don't be silly, Maggs. You know that sweater's merino wool."

They brought sausage patties back for the dogs. As Maggie leaned over to hand off the greasy treasure, Fluffy launched himself skyward and clocked her in the cheek with the top of his head. She gingerly touched her face.

"That'll leave a mark," she said ruefully.

They fed, walked, and loaded up the dogs, then turned up Highway 28. They had agreed to look for the yellow blob on their gold map located at Parsons Mountain. It was deep in the National Forest, but it appeared to have public access. They turned onto a forest service road where a sign indicated Parsons Mountain OHV trail. Maggie wasn't sure what OHV meant, but if there was a marked trail, she figured there would be less chance of getting accidentally shot.

Once they crossed the second 4 wheeler trail, Maggie decided that the O must stand for offroad and the V for vehicle. The H was anybody's guess. She hoped they would find a regular hiking trail farther down the road.

After about five minutes more of driving they arrived at a spur going to their left off forestry road 515. There, on the right side of the road, across from the spur was a trailhead. They spotted a van parked on a wide spot at the intersection, with two men unloading camping gear. Cher and Maggie immediately recognized one of the men from the Thursday evening news report.

Maggie pulled up next to the van and rolled down her window. "Excuse me, could you help us with directions? I'm Maggie and this is my friend, Cher. We're looking for gold. Have you seen any streams nearby where we can pan?"

The man with the brown hair and glasses answered for them. "Hello. I'm Paul and this is my faculty advisor, Sam. I've seen a stream that crosses the road about one half mile up. It may be a good place to pan."

"Thanks! We've been looking for a gold mine, but if we can't find one we'll have to settle for a stream."

"But there are gold mines right here! If you take the left fork at this trailhead and walk about five minutes you'll come across four old mine shafts. The openings are surrounded by chain link fences, so you can't miss them."

Cher looked relieved. "Thank goodness we found a place to dig, otherwise you'll have me out looking for old soap."

Maggie cocked her head as she looked at Paul. "Was that you who I saw on the news Thursday? You had a car accident in a pillow factory?"

Paul blushed. "I didn't expect to become a celebrity. I hope I haven't wasted my fifteen minutes of fame on a freak accident."

"Don't be so modest." Maggie said. "I'd give it closer to a week before people forget all about it. Thank you for your help! I think we'll start with some panning today."

Maggie backed the jeep onto the main road and headed for the stream. As she pulled to the side of the road behind a small pickup truck, she looked in dismay at what could only charitably be called a creek in an open field—more of a wide ditch, really. The road had descended from the spur, leaving them in a small valley with a runoff ditch from the surrounding hills. Two men were squatting at the edge about 100 feet down-ditch from the road.

"I call the paella pan," Cher piped in.

"No fair. The wok has deeper sides, so it will require more sloshing. That's going to be hell on my shoulder."

"Sorry, darling, but repetitive yank syndrome from walking your dog in a squirrel infested park is not recognized by the American Medical Association."

"C'mon," Maggie pleaded. "I can get a note from my chiropractor."

Cher stepped out of the jeep and turned back in to face Maggie. "I'm afraid that 'dibs' will have to remain inviolable. You wouldn't want to set a legal precedent that could rock the courts for years to come."

"When you put it that way," Maggie grumbled. She popped the back hatch and got out.

The men below were staring unabashedly at Maggie and Cher, with a definite look of appreciation in their eyes. Maggie leaned into the jeep to tie bright bandanas around the necks of Buddy and Fluffy. The dogs were already crawling over the backseat, shaking with anticipation, and intent on that big open space beyond the human who was blocking them in. As soon as Maggie stepped aside, two balls of fur exploded from the back of the jeep.

The men jumped up and staggered backward as the dogs charged across the field and leapt joyfully into the water a few feet up-ditch from them. Maggie was still apologizing as the men picked up their gear and trudged past her to the truck. Their mood appeared to be as dark as their mud-splattered pants.

"Well," Cher said, as she pulled out a package of standard-issue yellow rubber gloves, "that just leaves more gold for us."

She pulled the gloves on, snapped the cuff lightly, and handed the other pair with the paella pan to Maggie, as the truck roared away. "I'm going to want to see that note from your chiropractor, darling."

"It's just on the other side of this ridge," Paul explained. "I think the original entrance was covered by a landslide long before the 1852 gold rush in the area."

Sam took his cue and started up the trail from the road spur. As they passed the four vertical mine shafts, he strained to see as far down as he could, but the chain link prevented him from getting close enough to judge the depth. A sign indicated that this was the Parsons Mountain goldmine.

They trudged up the trail another 20 minutes until they made the summit. Spurred on by the excitement of discovery, they didn't even pause at the top to admire the breathtaking hills covered in the gold of autumn leaves. The trail going down the other side turned into a gully between ever steepening banks. They soon reached the bottom to find a large clearing surrounded by southern pine forest. The ground was packed solid, still showing traces of the grooves and ruts from ore cars and wagons in its petrified surface.

For 500 feet along the hillside to the right of the trail's end, walls of granite rose above the clearing. Roughly in the middle of this wall was what they came for. A mine entrance stood, guarded only by a stretch of chain link fence. The men dropped their camping gear, pulled out their lanterns and hurried to the fence. On the right side of the mouth of the mineshaft, there was plenty of room to slide in between the end of the fence and the rock wall. One hundred yards in, Paul passed a shaft leading to the right without slowing down. Sam was looking down constantly, trying not to trip over the rails for the ore cars.

The dust they kicked up hung suspended, reflecting in the glow of their lanterns.

Sam had totally lost track of how quickly they were descending under the mountain, when Paul stopped short. He was shining his light at the base of the wall on their right, where Sam could make out a dark horizontal seam. At the center of the seam was a low opening just large enough for a man to crawl through.

"This is the entrance to the natural cave," Paul said.

"That's going to be a tight squeeze."

"Maybe we'll need to set a weight limit for students who want to dig. What do you think, Sam, you want to go first?"

"I'll take a pass on that, since you know the caves."

Paul got on his hands and knees and crawled through the opening, followed closely by Sam. The entrance opened up after just a few feet. They emerged into a large vaulted cavern.

"I don't know how long that gap has been there between the mine and the caves, but it's the only access I've found so far." Paul's voice echoed through the chamber.

They heard the sound of running water, and headed in that direction. Here and there, splotches of white paint on the cave floor marked the way.

Sam brushed the dirt off his pant legs. "How did you find this place?"

"I overheard some hunters in town talking about the old mine. When I asked them about caves in the area, they got really quiet. It was a 12 year-old boy standing nearby who piped up with the story of the old Indian burial ground under the mountain. He said that during the rainy season, water from the cave would sometimes flow into the mine through fissures in the wall. A few weeks ago, he and his friends ran into a nest of rattlers in the mine, so they're steering clear of it."

"Eastern diamondback," Sam sighed. "Sure don't want to run into any of those. You might have told me that before I started crawling around in the mine."

"Would that have stopped you?"

Sam laughed. "They'd have to be damn big snakes to keep me out for long."

Chapter Seventeen

They were only twenty minutes into their panning and Maggie's back was already sore. Cher wasn't complaining, but she looked a little stiff as she swished the water around the bottom of the wok.

"So tell me again why we're doing this," Maggie asked.

"It's the gold fever they talk about, like in *Treasure of the Sierra Madre.*"

"I think you actually have to find gold before you get gold fever."

Cher removed one rubber glove and massaged the back of her neck. "Give it time, we'll be at each others' throats soon enough."

"I don't think I brought ibuprofin. Is vodka considered a suitable analgesic?"

Just then, Fluffy spotted a tempting looking stick in the water next to Maggie. Fluffy had a number of vices, the worst of which involved eating poop. Not far down the list was his addiction to sticks. He especially loved the rotten, crumbling variety. This one was muddy with slimy grass streamers tangled around the end. Fluffy had the classic Rottweiler build: barrel-chested and solid. He was not light on his feet. Maggie presented an inconsequential obstacle between him and his prize.

"Oof!"

Her unlady-like grunt was cut short by a mouth-full of muddy water as she hurtled head first into the ditch. Cher hurried to her side to help lift her up. Maggie's hair was dripping around her face, and the front of her sweatshirt was streaked with grass stains from the bank.

"Darling!" Cher couldn't help laughing. "You seem to be having a little problem with gravity the last few days. We need to get you cleaned up."

Maggie stared daggers at Fluffy, now lying peacefully in the grass, chewing on his stick. She headed a few feet upstream to find clear water, undisturbed by Fluffy's exuberance, and proceeded to wash up, while trying to blow mud out of her nose. "We came here to find gold, and I'm not going home empty-handed."

Maggie marched back to the jeep, where she wiped her face and scrubbed at her hair with the muddy dog's towel. It did little more than smear the dirt around. "Did I get any on me?"

Cher just laughed, picked up her wok, and settled back into the task at hand.

Maggie had brought a plastic sandwich bag to store the gold that they would recover from the stream. Another hour of hunching over the ditch had done nothing to fill the bag.

Fluffy was stretched out in the grass, on his back, legs in the air. Buddy was snuggled up next to his side. Both dogs were twitching with their satisfied dreams.

Cher stood up and stretched. "Could we please, please, *please* call it a day?"

Maggie was no less anxious to give up on the day's adventure. "I'm hungry. I wonder where we could get a chili dog and a chocolate milkshake in this one-horse town?"

"Um, I didn't see any roadside diners on this end of town. That just leaves us with the same place we had breakfast."

"Well, I'm starved. Let's go get some hot dogs before we head back to the motel. At the moment, I'd rather be full than dry."

Cher called for the dogs as they started back to the jeep. It took a good ten minutes to hold them still long enough to wipe them down with the damp towel. When they reached the diner, they ordered chili dogs for themselves, and hot dogs for Buddy and Fluffy. Fluffy was no connoisseur, but Buddy preferred ketchup and relish on his. Since it was already late afternoon, they decided to pick up snacks on the way back to the motel, rather than go back out for dinner later. They were both too tired and sore to go to the inn.

Maggie took the bed closest to the bathroom, a precaution left over from her pre-surgery days. The bladder suspension had two effects: she no longer soiled herself every time she sneezed; and she now peed sideways to the right. Sometimes she wondered if the coreolis effect held true for urination. Would she pee to the left in the southern hemisphere? Since Cher had never had children, her pelvic sling muscles hadn't been stretched like a sweater on Jane Mansfield. She was content to take the bed nearest the windows.

Maggie had showered, put on an oversized t-shirt, and done her best to rinse the grass stains off her clothes. Now as she munched on Cheetos and flipped through the

TV channels, she realized that Cher had been in the bathroom for a long time.

Maggie went to the bathroom and put her ear to the door. Inside she could hear what sounded like muffled weeping. She knocked gently. "Cher, what's the matter, honey? Do you want to talk about it?"

Cher opened the door, her face blotchy and a wad of toilet paper in her hand. She blew her nose, none too delicately and walked over to sit on her bed. Maggie sat down next to her and put an arm around her shoulders. They sat silently for a minute.

"Howard may have been a hound dog," Cher began without preamble, "but he's always taken good care of his son."

"But Cher, you never had any ... Oh my God! Are you saying that Howard had a child with some other woman?"

Cher scooted back on the bed and crossed her legs. "Come on darling, as much as he played around, I'm surprised he doesn't have a whole flock of children. Dora Lakeland was Howard's secretary back in the early eighties. They had to work late together on many occasions. It didn't take a rocket scientist to figure out what kind of work they were doing. I rarely went to the office, and I never voiced my suspicions. One day, I dropped in to see if Howard was free for lunch. There was Dora, seven months pregnant. She brought me a cup of coffee, chattering about the pregnancy. The little witch knew that I'd had no success at getting pregnant, and she seemed to be lording it over me. I just sat numbly, drinking my coffee and praying that the child wasn't Howard's."

"... but it was Howard's?"

"Dora dropped off some paperwork at the house one Sunday shortly after giving birth. She brought the baby with her. I held her little boy while she went to Howard's den to give him the papers. When she returned she made some comment about how the baby took after his father. Her eyes were sparkling with malice as she said it. Just then, Howard walked into the living room and saw me holding the baby. He absolutely went white before my eyes. That's when I knew.

The thing is, in that moment, I wasn't angry with Howard—I was jealous of Dora. She was able to give Howard what I couldn't. No matter how involved Howard chose to be in his son's life, the bitter reality was that the baby who was sucking on my finger should have been my child."

They were both sniffling by now, so Maggie got up and brought the whole roll of toilet paper and the plastic cups from the bathroom. She snagged the four airline size bottles of vodka they had brought so they could celebrate finding the motherlode.

Cher blotted her tears with the toilet paper. "I know it sounds crazy, but I wanted that child. I imagined what it would be like to play pat-a-cake and peek-a-boo; to tuck him in each night. I worried about whether or not Dora really loved him like I could."

They both took a healthy drink of the liquor before Maggie asked, "Why now? It must be close to 30 years since you found out. If Dora has been unkind to you all these years, I'm going to go rip her hair out!"

"No, I haven't heard from Dora, but I kept track of her son until his teens. Once, I even went to his school play. I sat in the back, and it seemed like he was the only boy on stage. I couldn't take my eyes off him. Maggie, the young man who gave us directions to the mine: that was Paul Lakeland. I hadn't made the connection until Thursday, when we saw him on the news and you said that he looked like Howard. I was horrified that he might have died in that crash. I still have a special place in my heart for him, but I could never bring myself to intrude in his life."

Maggie patted Cher's knee, and they polished off the vodka in silence.

Chapter Eighteen

His feet were cold, his hands were cold, and his heart was hammering in his chest as he kept watch over the campsite from the treeline. It was 3:00 AM, and there was no sign of movement. The moon kept playing hide and seek behind the clouds, casting intermittent lacy patterns on the hard-packed earth of the clearing. For now, the moon was obscured and the campsite was nearly invisible in the darkness.

This was different. As soon as he picked up the gun, all the rules had changed. There was something fundamentally wrong about simply unzipping the tent and shooting a man in his sleep … so he waited.

A flashlight snapped on in the tent and the flap opened. Paul Lakeland stepped out into the dark, a roll of toilet paper in one hand, and a flashlight in the other. Bear ducked down as a beam of light swiveled in his direction. He would have to wait to fire until Lakeland was in point blank range, since the form behind the bright light was little more than a barely discernable silhouette. He assumed a sniper's crouch and shouldered his rifle, checking the sights out of habit. It was too late when he remembered that he hadn't changed to the night scope. *Stupid!* He had a powerful scope, but it was useless in the full dark. Lakeland stumbled, half asleep to the tree line, about two car lengths to his left.

Bear hesitated, wondering again if he could really kill a man in cold blood. This time he would be looking him in the eye. His hands were clammy with sweat as he chambered the round, took a deep breath, and pulled the trigger on the exhale. There was no ear-shattering explosion; not even a click. He checked the safety, then realized that the bullet had jammed before entering the chamber.

"Son of a bitch!" he whispered.

His window of opportunity was closing. As Lakeland pulled up his pants and turned back toward the tent, Bear jumped up. Without making a conscious decision, he gripped the rifle by the barrel and closed the distance between them. He didn't remember swinging, but he clearly heard the hollow *thunk* as the solid wood of the rifle butt hit Lakeland's head with enough force to knock him off his feet. Lakeland only stayed down a moment before he was on his feet and half running, half stumbling toward the tent. His attempt at flight earned him a brutal flying tackle.

Bear dropped the rifle so he would have both hands free for the take-down. As soon as Lakeland hit the ground, Bear jumped up, his eyes darting around, looking for anything that could be used as a weapon … then he saw the rock hammer lying on the camp table a few feet away. Lakeland was on his hands and knees, still struggling to get back up when the chisel end of the hammer connected. Bear's ears were thundering with the wild beating of his heart as he felt the hammer penetrate hair, and skin, and bone. He still held the hammer as the body went limp, slumping chest-down to the ground. Only the head, still impaled on the chisel, arched upward, suspended like some macabre marionette. He lowered the head and placed one foot on it for leverage, as he wiggled the hammer free. He could feel the bile rising in his throat, coating his mouth with the taste of sour beer.

The moon was starting to peek out enough that he could make out his rifle and Lakeland's flashlight near the treeline. As he walked over and picked them up, the clouds parted, flooding the clearing with light. He straightened and turned to look at the lifeless body, with blood staining the blonde hair. His heart skipped a beat as his brain fought to make sense of what he was seeing. *Blond? Blond hair?*

Bear's mind groped for any possible explanation, but there was only one.

His hand trembled more with each step he took towards the body. He crouched down and curled his fingers into the hair, mindless of the sticky, wet blood. He turned the head to look into the unblinking open eyes. Even without using the flashlight, he could tell that they were an extraordinary shade of blue.

He killed the wrong man!

He released the hair and rocked back on his heels, landing on his ass with a thud.

Maggie woke at 5:00 AM and pumped her fist in a silent "hurrah." After Cher's revelation last night, she hadn't expected to get any sleep. "Vodka - one; insomnia - zero." She quietly chanted.

She crept to the bathroom, blinking in the unforgiving glare of light bouncing off white tile and porcelain. As she exited the bathroom, she glanced at Cher, hoping that the noise hadn't wakened her. Two dogs were passed out on the bedspread, but there was no sign of Cher.

Maggie scurried around the tiny room like a hamster on crack, looking behind and under the beds, in the closet, and behind the shower curtain in the bathtub. It was then that she realized that Cher's purse was also missing.

She took a deep breath and forced herself to calm down. Yes, Cher had been upset, but she wouldn't do something stupid. She had obviously needed to go out for some reason. Cher must have intended to be back before Maggie awoke, since she hadn't seen a note during her frantic search.

Maggie's dead-in-the-ditchaphobia kicked in with a vengeance. She rushed unthinking into the bathroom, tugging the clothes off the shower rod. At least they had dried during the night. Her car keys were not on the dresser, but as she stepped out into the parking lot, there was her jeep, two spaces down from where she had left it yesterday. As she approached the jeep, she was weak with relief to see Cher reclining, asleep in the driver's seat.

Maggie rapped loudly on the window until Cher turned her head and painfully pried her eyes open. She raised the seat and opened the door. A half bottle of cheap wine rolled off the edge of the seat and struck the pavement with a crash, sending liquor and glass flying under the jeep.

Heedless of the glass crunching under her shoes, Maggie leaned in the open door and gave Cher a clumsy hug. "Oh, sweetheart, I'm so glad you're all right. When you weren't in the room I was afraid something had happened to you."

Cher looked sheepishly at the ground. "I'm so sorry, Maggs. Some of that splashed onto your car door."

"What are you doing out here?"

"I couldn't sleep. I remembered a liquor store just off Main Street, so I went out for some wine. Unfortunately, I forgot to take my key card. I didn't want to pound on the door and wake you up."

Maggie swung her hand as if to smack Cher on the side of the head. "Idiot! I would have been happy to let you in. I'll go find a broom. Here's the key card. Why don't you go get a towel and wipe up the door?"

"I really am sorry for worrying you, darling. I just needed some time to think."

Maggie had never known Cher to withdraw when distressed. Her friend had always been very direct, eager to share her joys and her pain. Now, suddenly Cher was a woman of mystery. Maggie looked at the wine label lying stuck to the broken glass. Cabernet Sauvignon? It was worse than she thought! Cher was not a wine snob, but she really disliked dry wine. Isn't there some rule that you might have a problem if you drink a vintage that you hate?

"I hope we don't get pulled over today with the car smelling like a distillery." Maggie wrinkled her nose. "Two women, a deserted highway, and a small town cop. It has Stephen King written all over it."

Cher laughed. "Ooh, small backwoods town stereotyping. Now you're starting to sound like me. Don't try to tell me that you weren't all kinds of freaked out when we went for the venison!"

"I was just worried about getting trampled. You're faster than I am."

The dogs slept through all the comings and goings of the clean-up, and only revived when they heard the rattle of food dishes.

As they walked the dogs, Maggie kept looking at Cher for any signs of distress. "You know, we can just head home now if you'd like."

"Really darling, I'm over it. Besides, we haven't been here long enough to find any gold. I think I could get a pretty good story out of that."

Cher was about to get more than she bargained for.

Chapter Nineteen

By 10:00 a.m. Maggie and Cher were hiking up the hillside of Parson's Mountain, while looking intently for any gold nuggets on the ground. They had returned to the place Paul had suggested the day before, and had no trouble finding the mine shafts, which were little more than four deep holes surrounded by chain link fence.

"I don't see any gold nuggets," Cher said. "I don't even see any rocks. There could be enough gold under our feet to fill Fort Knox, and we would never know it."

"Yeah, I hadn't really counted on all the fall leaves on the ground."

Cher stopped and scanned the hillside. There was little undergrowth, so the trail was only barely discernible from the rest of the forest floor. The air was scented with the fresh smell of pine, and the musty smell of decaying foliage.

"It really is beautiful, you know. It looks like the whole forest floor is painted with red and gold."

Maggie merely grunted.

Cher was carrying a backpack with water and box lunches from the inn, while Maggie carried their toolbox.

"Cher, remind me again, was fun anywhere in the equation when we made our hobby list?"

"Have you lost interest already? It's not too late to turn back."

"If this tool kit gets any heavier, I'm likely to lose my will to live. Let's keep heading up the hill. There must be rocks somewhere on this god-forsaken mountain."

When they reached the top, their sour moods melted away. Even Maggie had to stop and whistle appreciatively. The hills below were ablaze with color, and seemed to go on forever.

They turned left and continued along the ridge until they found what they were looking for—a huge rock outcropping. There were stones of all sizes littering the ground. They set up their base of operations near a large boulder. Maggie started picking up likely looking rocks and handing them to Cher to crack open.

Cher swore as she hit her finger for the second time with the rock hammer. "Oh, tart cookies! I broke a nail."

"Let it all out, Cher. Are we having a little problem with eye-hand coordination, sweetie?"

"We're still too hung over to see straight."

"Would you like to trade jobs for awhile? I can crack and you can gather. It would probably be safer."

"I don't know. You haven't exactly exhibited swan-like grace yourself this weekend."

"Point taken." Maggie smiled.

They traded jobs. Cher took over aimlessly wandering about, picking up rocks here and there.

Minutes after Maggie started cracking rocks, she gave a soft laugh. "You know, sweetie, back in the day, breaking up rocks was left to prisoners in jail. We actually volunteered for hard labor."

"I know, my back is sore from bending over, and we haven't even dug a single hole. We wouldn't last a day in the hoosegow."

Some of the rocks Cher found had flakes that sparkled gold in the sun. Finally, they had something to put into their sandwich bags. Maggie didn't want to head home that afternoon with nothing to show for their efforts.

The dogs had been running circles around them as they hiked up the mountain, and were now sleeping on the sun-warmed rock shelf. When Cher opened the backpack to retrieve the box lunches they had purchased at the inn, Buddy and Fluffy snapped to immediate attention.

The girls drank in the view as they ate their lunch.

"You know, darling," Cher said, as she wiped some mustard off her chin, "we still have to get these rocks down to the car. I can only carry so much in the backpack, and the toolbox is already full of gear. Maybe we should start heading back."

"You'll get no arguments from me."

They packed up and retraced their steps along the top of the ridge. It felt like they had been walking a long time. Had they overshot the trailhead? With all the leaves on the ground, could they have missed it?

To their left, they heard a crashing in the bushes, followed by a loud baying sound. Buddy and Fluffy barked joyfully and took off like a shot down the hill.

"What is that?" Cher asked, a look of panic in her eyes. "Buddy, come here, boy!"

The baying grew louder and closer, until the bushes erupted with Buddy and Fluffy, followed by a mass of beagles. A big old bloodhound brought up the rear of the group.

As soon as the unruly pack reached Maggie and Cher, they came to an abrupt halt. The beagles quieted down and started an odd dance in which the dogs were all trying to sniff each other at the same time. Maggie was getting dizzy trying to count heads.

Cher voiced the obvious question. "Where are their owners? Please tell me these poor dogs aren't just running wild?"

More crashing in the woods answered her question, as two men emerged from the trees. They were dressed head to toe in camouflage and carrying rifles. Without missing a beat, they both tipped their hunting caps, as if they had met in the park.

"Ladies, lovely day today," said the taller of the two.

He had a square jawline, dusted with a two-day growth of beard. Bright blue eyes sparkled, as if he was enjoying a private joke.

The other hunter was only a little taller than Cher. Bright red hair peeked out from under his cap, and he spoke with a slow comfortable drawl.

"Why, Dan, I think we need to git these poor ol' dogs' eyes checked. They's supposed to be chasin' hogs."

Maggie and Cher hadn't moved. Cher leaned over and whispered, "I've heard what they do to ..."

"Well," Maggie broke in, "we seem to have found your dogs."

"More like the other way around, ma'am," Said the red-haired man. "I'm forgettin' my manners. My name's Andy, and this is my buddy Dan."

"Hi, my name's Maggie, and this is my friend Cher. We were just out here doing a little prospecting."

Dan's eyebrows flew up. "For gold? I'm afraid these parts are pretty well picked over. Nobody's found any gold in a long time."

Andy swept his arm around and said, "You can pick up any old rock here and find pyrite—that's fool's gold—but there ain't no real gold left."

Cher shrugged out of her backpack and let it drop to the ground. The dogs nearest her jumped back at the sudden thump of the bag. "You mean the rocks I've been lugging around are just … rocks?"

"Like as not," Andy said. "Anybody kin make that mistake."

Without a word, Cher squatted down, unzipped the pack and started pulling out handfuls of sandwich bags. She merely dropped them on the ground.

"Here, let me help you with that," Dan said as he laid down his rifle. He squatted down next to Cher and started opening bags, dumping the once precious rocks onto the hillside.

Maggie and Andy stood by awkwardly as they finished the task.

"That should lighten your load some," Dan said. "Are you ladies planning on staying out here for awhile? It's not too safe wandering around during hunting season."

"We were actually just getting ready to head home," Cher said. "Thanks for rescuing us from public humiliation and ridicule. We would have been a long time living this one down."

Dan tipped his hat. "Happy to oblige, ma'am. Can you find your way back to the road okay? The trail down the hill is about fifty feet over there."

"We'll be fine," Maggie said. "Thanks for your help."

Andy gave a whistle for the dogs, and the men started walking along the ridge in the direction the girls had come from. As one, the pack loped after the men. Buddy and Fluffy took a few steps in that direction, but turned to follow Maggie and Cher as they walked away toward the trail. Within minutes, they were out of sight, running ahead on the trail. As victories went, having the dogs behave themselves was about as good as it was going to get.

Maggie and Cher caught up to the dogs near the mine pits. They were nosing about in a curious circular pattern around one of the shafts. Suddenly, they both started barking in frenzied unison. Runoff from the rain had created a trough that ran under one of the fences. The depression it formed was easily deep enough for Buddy, who wasted no time in darting through the gap. Fluffy could get his shoulders through, but his upraised backside prevented him from continuing on. He seemed unaware that he would have to get down on his belly to squeeze through. Cher was beside herself with worry that Buddy might fall into the pit, but nothing could entice him back from the edge.

"If I pull this fence up, do you think you can get under?" Maggie asked. "I would have to have bone mass surgically removed to squeeze through."

Maggie pulled on the lower edge for all she was worth, and managed to bend the fence up ever so slightly. It was enough for Cher, who immediately squeezed through on her belly, and then rushed over to grab Buddy's collar. She peered over the edge.

Cher could hardly make herself heard over the dogs' continued wild barking. She shoved Buddy under the fence to the waiting arms of Maggie. "Could you hand me the flashlight? It's too dark in there, and I'd like to see what's gotten into the dogs."

Maggie fished the flashlight out of the toolbox and handed it to Cher. Light in hand, she knelt by the side of the pit. The click of the flashlight was followed almost immediately by a scream. She dropped the light into the pit and madly scrambled back away from the edge. She was white as a sheet and crawling under the fence before Maggie could pull up the bottom edge. The seat of Cher's pants snagged on the fence, and she struggled to free herself. Maggie managed to hold Buddy's collar in one hand and haul on the fence with the other. Cher shot out of the trough, pulling herself up to her hands and knees. Maggie put a one-armed hug around her trembling friend as she heaved up her lunch. The intensity of the barking was making Maggie's head spin.

"What did you see?" she shouted.

"There's somebody ... a man down there. His eyes were open, but he wasn't moving! Do you think...?"

Maggie let go of her friend and pulled her cell phone out of her jacket pocket. "I hope 911 works in the wilderness."

Realizing that nobody on the phone would hear her over the barking, she passed Buddy off to Cher and jogged up the hill to make the call. "Great!" she thought.

"I just sprang a leak." She silently thanked the makers of panty liners and dialed the police.

"There's a man in a hole." She blurted into the phone.

"911, please state the nature of your emergency."

"He might be dead!"

"Who is this?"

"I'm Maggie, and Cher found him and dropped her flashlight, and the dogs won't stop barking!"

"Calm down, ma'am. Do you know how he got in the hole?"

Maggie stared at the phone in disbelief. "Does it matter? What if he's not dead? We've got to get him out of there, now!"

The operator gave a loud sigh. "Please tell me where you are."

Maggie gave the directions.

"It will take about 45 minutes to get emergency vehicles to your location. Please don't leave the area until the police have had a chance to talk to you."

Chapter Twenty

Jonathan was at the inn wolfing down his macaroni and cheese while looking over some legal briefs. If he hurried, he could still get in some fishing. Two McCormick County deputies were seated at the table next to his when the call came in. Mike Henderson looked longingly at his half eaten hamburger as he acknowledged the call on his walkie-talkie. He shook his head slowly and signed off.

"Whatcha got, Mike?" Jonathan asked.

"Timmy fell in the well. Actually, some damned fool tourist managed to fall into one of the mineshafts. We got a call in this morning from a camper saying his friend went missing last night. This might be our missing person."

Jonathan had plenty of wealthy clients in Columbia, so he didn't need to chase ambulances ... but he was intrigued. His pole and tackle box were in his trunk, so he could go straight to the river from the mine. "Mind if I follow you out there?"

"Suit yourself. Just stay out of the way."

"Where you headed?"

"The Parsons Mountain goldmine, off forestry road 515."

"Yeah, I know the place. I'll catch up to you."

Mike and his partner, Bobby, scooped up their leftover hamburgers, threw some money on the table, and headed for the door. Jonathan finished his lunch, paid the waiter, and hurried out to his Mercedes. A drive that took most people forty-five minutes, he could make in a half hour. He just wanted to make sure that he gave Mike and Bobby a good head start. They probably wouldn't appreciate it if he passed them on the way.

It was chaos. The front of Cher's clothes were coated in dirt from her tight squeeze, and there was a rip in the seat of her jeans. Maggie's jeans were sprinkled with grit from standing in the fallout zone of Fluffy's attempts to dig under the fence. At least his futile attempts had the effect of deepening the trench, and his massive body was blocking the way, thwarting any chance for Buddy to worm his way back in. Cher had run to the car for the leashes, and they managed to wrestle the little mutts into the jeep, where they finally stopped barking. The dogs immediately slipped into a coma, and didn't even wake up when Bobby and Mike arrived—sirens blaring.

Maggie and Cher were waiting by the jeep so they could direct the police. Truth be told, they were also creeped out at the thought of waiting around near a possible corpse. An ambulance arrived on the tail of the police. While the EMTs were gathering their gear, a dusty Mercedes pulled over just down the road from the emergency vehicles.

Maggie was trying to explain in a tumble of words what had happened, but the taller of the two policemen shushed her, as if she were an annoying child. Because Cher seemed the more calm of the two at this point, Mike turned his attention to her. He seemed slightly distracted from his questions as he visually examined Cher's front to make sure she was uninjured. At least that's what it looked like to Maggie. The EMTs were lining up behind the policemen to check her out and make sure she wasn't hurt as well.

"I'm fine. Could we please get going?"

It finally registered with Maggie that the fine looking man standing behind the police was that lawyer they had met at the inn. His hair was slightly disheveled, which did nothing to detract from his rugged good looks. She was surprised to see him there, but her speculation came to an abrupt halt as Cher took the lead heading up the trail. The men fell in behind her, apparently concerned that she might have injured her backside as well. Maggie brought up the rear.

Extricating the fallen man was a comedy of errors. Apparently the shaft was too narrow for a stretcher. They lowered a man down who rigged a harness around the victim, but as they attempted to raise him, the limp body kept banging into protruding rocks, dumping stones and dirt onto the EMT waiting 20 feet below. With dead weight on the other end, the rope slipped twice from the fingers of the other EMT. "Hey, guys. Could I get a hand over here?"

The space between the fence and lip of the pit was too narrow for more than one man, so they strung the end of the rope over the fence and Jonathan, Mike, and Bobby joined in on the macabre tug of war.

The victim was wearing only thermal underwear. When he finally reached the top, he was flopped over like a rag doll, and his long johns had snagged on several rocks and a protruding tree root, dragging the underwear to pool around his knees. He emerged from the pit with his backside exposed to the sky in an impressive full moon.

Shock and hysteria took over, which started Maggie giggling. Soon she was laughing so hard that she was crying, and her pants were wet again. *Damn!*

As the other EMT was raised to the surface, a man dressed in an argyle sweater and blue jeans huffed up the hill, heading straight for them. He was a little shorter than Maggie, round, and balding. He pushed his wire rim glasses up his nose as he approached the group. By now, the body was lying next to the pit, and the EMTs had pronounced him dead, which sobered Maggie up immediately. Sweater guy nodded at the ladies as he proceeded over to talk to the policemen.

"Do we know who he is?" he started without preamble.

"Hey, Carl," Mike greeted him. "We believe he's a camper who went missing last night. We'll have to bring his buddy in to identify the body. That's all I've got right now."

"Who found him?"

"Those ladies over there. They're pretty shook up."

"Shaken" Carl automatically corrected him. "I'll just have a word with them if you don't mind."

"Knock yourself out, boss."

Carl walked over and introduced himself to Maggie and Cher. "Hi. I'm Carl Chambers, editor of the McCormick Messenger. I understand that you ladies found the body."

Maggie cringed at hearing the word, "body" instead of "man."

"Actually, our dogs found him," Cher answered. "Oh, I'm Cher Anderson and this is my friend, Maggie Gorski."

He was already scribbling in a notepad. "Pleased to meet you. Do you know who he is?"

Maggie was distracted, watching the EMTs struggle to stuff the limp body under the fence. His arms and legs seemed to have a mind of their own, getting tangled repeatedly and catching on the barbs at the bottom of the chain link. She almost got the giggles again until she got a good look at the dried blood coating his face and matted in his hair.

Cher said, "We met him on the road down there yesterday. I can't remember his name. He was with Paul."

"Paul, who?"

Cher was flustered. How Paul fit into her personal life was none of this man's business. "He said his name was Paul Lakeland."

Carl looked at Cher appraisingly, then moved on. "When did you discover the body?"

"Sam" Maggie said triumphantly. "He said his name was Sam. We found him about two hours ago, when Cher's dog snuck under the fence and ran to the edge of the hole. He was jumping around and going nuts, so Cher went in after him. That's when she saw him … Sam. The police got here a little over an hour ago, I'd say. They just got him out of the hole."

Maggie ran out of juice as she looked over somberly at the stretcher. The EMTs were just picking up Sam's body to take him down the hill to the waiting ambulance. Jonathan walked over to stand with the girls. Whether to comfort, protect, or eavesdrop, Maggie wasn't sure.

"Maggie and Cher are probably pretty tired, Carl. Can the questions wait?"

"No can do. I've got a county rezoning meeting this evening. It's liable to go late. Those windbags will dither around for at least an hour before they get to the point."

"I'm a journalist," Cher said brightly. "I could write up the account and drop it by your office."

Carl seemed to make his decision on the spot. "Give me a clean story and I'll print it as is. Great angle: an eyewitness perspective. Could you drop it off first thing tomorrow morning? We're the only red semi-circular awning on Main Street. You can't miss it."

"The one right across the train tracks from the inn?" Cher asked, trying not to bounce on the balls of her feet.

"That's the place. Here's my cell number if you need to reach me before then. Where are you ladies staying?"

"We're at the Sleepytime Motel. Room 107. Oh, wait. We were going home this afternoon."

"You want to give him your social security number while you're at it?" Maggie asked with a grin. "We can stay another night. I'll call Ted and let him know."

Mike had walked over at the tail end of the conversation. "Actually, I'd like to talk with you ladies later at the station. Could you come in around five?"

"Could we get something to eat first, maybe come around six?" Maggie asked.

Jonathan jumped on the opportunity. "Why don't I treat you ladies to dinner at the inn, then we can go to the station together. Wouldn't hurt to have an attorney around if they break out the rubber hoses."

Cher's eyes got round, until she realized it was a joke. "That would be really nice. We could meet you at the inn around five."

"It's a date," Jonathan said with a twinkle in his eye. "Until then." He gave an exaggerated bow before he started down the hill.

Chapter Twenty-one

"The fall isn't what killed him," she said simply.

Elizabeth Matson had just finished her evening run when she got the call. She hadn't even showered, because of the urgency of the situation. The cadavers weren't going to care if she was less than perfectly groomed. It was past five by the time she had completed the preliminary examination. After hunching over the body for two hours, she was getting hungry … and cranky.

At twenty-eight years old, she could have been a Victoria's Secret swimsuit model—not what you would expect for a county coroner in rural South Carolina. Her luxurious chestnut hair was pulled back in a ponytail, and the geeky-looking black-rimmed safety glasses did nothing to detract from the beauty of her green eyes.

"What makes you say that, Liz?"

She took a small measure of satisfaction. If she was going to miss dinner, she'd make damn well sure that the sheriff missed his as well. She could legitimately call him in because of the nature of her findings, but she had to admit to a little revenge.

"Blunt force trauma was the cause of death, consistent with a fall of twenty feet. The bleeding and bruising around the laceration suggests that his heart didn't stop beating immediately, not unusual with blunt force trauma. When I shaved his head, I found additional bruising to the back of his head: consistent with a fall."

"But?"

"If the fall caused the bleeding and bruising to his head, there should be multiple bruises and contusions on his body, but I've got nada, zilch, bupkus."

"I love it when you talk dirty!" Artie said with a grin.

"Dry up, Smith!"

"So what does that tell you?"

"That the bruises and laceration to his head were made while his heart was still beating. He went into the mineshaft after his heart had stopped. Simply put, he was already dead when he fell into that hole.

He was hit in the back of the head at least once: probably a stunning blow, then struck with some sort of sharp instrument. The laceration penetrates the skull in a regular pattern. Since he couldn't have walked off the edge after he was dead, somebody threw him in there."

Artie whistled. "Looks like we got us a murder." He pulled out his walkie-talkie. "Bobby, get out to Lakeland's campsite and bring him back in here for questioning before he leaves town."

Artie walked to the door of the county morgue and shouted down the hall, "Mike!"

"Yeah."

"Call forensics in Columbia. I want them out at that campsite tonight. This has turned into a murder investigation."

"I'm on it!"

He turned back to Liz. "Do we have a time of death?"

"Between two-thirty and three-thirty this morning."

"How soon can you have the full report put together?"

Liz sighed. "I'll have it to you in the next few hours, if I don't pass out from hunger before that. I'll make a copy for the forensics team."

"You're the best, Liz!"

"Don't get used to it."

Artie Smith may not have fit most people's opinion of a handsome man, but he was an imposing figure. With his muscular frame and buzz cut, he looked like ex-Special Forces turned small town cop, which is exactly what he was. He met his wife, Carla at Clemson, and married her right out of college, before he was deployed to Desert Storm. After the service, he moved to McCormick to be close to her family.

This evening, Artie had met his match. He was getting a headache. Maggie and Cher had shown up promptly at six, chipper and looking forward to their first police interview. He was surprised to see Jonathan along with them, but hardly had a chance to voice his disapproval. Cher Anderson was asking as many questions as he was, having assigned herself as reporter to what had become a murder investigation. Jonathan was leaning against the wall next to the door, enjoying the whole circus.

As Cher continued her questions, taking copious notes, Artie wondered when he had lost control of the situation.

"I'll need the full name of the deceased," Cher said.

"We're withholding that information pending the notification of his family."

"Paul introduced him as his faculty advisor. A quick internet search will give me that information. Since you're probably notifying the family as we speak, and this story won't hit the newsstands for ..." she had to think. *Did Carl say when the next issue would be published?* "... awhile yet, why not just give me the name?"

"I'm the one asking the questions here," Artie reminded her.

"And I'm the press. If you're not forthcoming with general information on the murder investigation ... well, you can see how it might look like a police cover-up." She had no idea what they might be covering up, and was pretty certain that she was overstepping her bounds as a reporter.

Artie had missed dinner, and only fifteen minutes into the interview he was praying for the sweet release of death. "If you'll excuse me a moment, ladies."

He left the room to get some aspirin and check on the background stories for Maggie and Cher. He was anxious to finish taking their statements and get them out of his interrogation room.

Maggie looked around the small room. "I thought they would have a two-way mirror. Bummer!"

Jonathan walked around the table and sat in the chair recently vacated by Artie. "You girls have thrown our poor town sheriff for a loop," he said, with a smile. "I have to caution you, though, since this has turned into a murder investigation, all the rules are out the window. Artie is smart, and he can be as badass as they come. The simple fact that you found the body has you on the police radar. They're going to examine what you do and say with a fine-tooth comb. Our sheriff is probably out their verifying everything from your banking accounts to your shoe size as we speak."

Cher was doodling a picture of a stick figure man throwing another stick figure into a hole. She was apparently considering artwork for her headlining story. That left Maggie to think through the implications of their situation. "You don't think they suspect us of anything, do you?"

"It's their job to make connections. You and Cher are now two of the playing pieces in this game. Mark my words, Artie will ask you not to leave town for a few days. He can't make you stay, but he might threaten that it would slow down their investigation if you go home now. He'll imply that by staying, you'll be cleared of any suspicion faster."

"Are we seriously under suspicion?"

"You are officially 'persons of interest.'"

"Wow! That's not my first choice of ways to be interesting, but it's better than dancing on the bar at ladies night."

"I told you they'd throw us out," Cher said distractedly.

Jonathan gently pulled the pencil out of Cher's hand and placed it on the table next to her. "I'd like each of you to give me one dollar."

"Why?" they asked in unison.

"So that when Artie comes back in that door, you will have legal counsel with you. I can tell him where to get off if he starts asking inappropriate questions. I'm not a criminal lawyer, but I can watch your backs in here."

There were goose bumps on Maggie's arms as she pawed through her purse. "I seem to be a little short. Can you take seventy-eight cents and a breath mint? I've never needed a lawyer before. This is way cool!"

Cher handed Jonathan a dollar and turned her full attention on him. "This means we have client privilege to confidentiality?"

"Yep."

"I may need to take you up on that if things start getting out of hand."

"Why don't you stop by my office in the morning after you drop off your story. I'm just a few doors down from the Messenger. I can make you a cup of my world famous lousy coffee, and you can fill me in on anything you don't want the police to know about."

Cher pouted. "Damn! Now that you're my attorney, I guess that means no second date."

Jonathan laughed. "Please feel free to fire me as soon as this is sorted out!"

Maggie made a gagging noise. "Kill me now."

Chapter Twenty-two

Maggie would have liked to watch the Sunday night game, but the Panthers were on a bye week, and the Washington / Indianapolis game promised to be a rout. In the end, she pulled out her copy of *Pride and Prejudiced Vampires,* and planned to read herself to sleep. Cher was oblivious to everything going on around her as she worked on her story for the *Messenger.* They walked into the interrogation room that evening expecting to answer questions about an accident victim, and they left with a murder story.

Maggie found her place and tried to concentrate on a vampire attack on Charlotte Lucas. She rolled her eyes. "Oh, for heaven's sake," she thought, "who decided that this would be a good read for their book club?"

Generally, Maggie and Cher timed their attendance to the club for when they knew Julia Mackie would be serving her red velvet cake. Maggie felt her mouth water as she continued to read. Damn Pavlovian response! She dozed off and woke several times, lulled by the tapping of Cher's fingers flying across the keyboard. She had no idea what time it was when she realized that the tapping had stopped. Maggie opened her eyes a slit as Cher crawled into bed. "How's your story?"

"I'm thinking Pulitzer. Maggie?"

"What?" she yawned.

"We could solve this. Can you imagine what a story that would make?"

"That's nice," Maggie said, her eyes drooping again.

Cher wasn't sure that she would be able to get to sleep, but soon the rhythmic breathing of her roomie and the dogs relaxed her. She drifted off thinking about Jonathan, and wondering what benefits came as part of his representation.

"Could he have been any more obvious?" Donna asked. As head of the crime scene investigation unit out of Columbia, there was very little that still surprised her. She was a bulldog of a woman in both appearance and temperament. She was a stickler for details, and her crew rarely questioned her orders.

"Why would he leave the murder weapon sitting out in plain view, with blood and hair still visible on the chisel? The coroner's report indicated that the shape of the wound suggested something with a small but thick blade. Check it for prints, Joe. I wonder if he even bothered to wipe the hammer after he used it. Ray, as soon as the dog gets here, I want you to follow the trail to the pit and look for footprints, or anything that might have been dropped along the way. The ground here is too hard packed for prints, and the area around the pit is contaminated from the rescue workers and police."

They worked through the night, bagging clothing, sleeping bags, and the tent; checking the perimeter of the campsite for any possible discarded items. They had a crew at the mine shaft as well, but they had come up empty, other than a flashlight in the pit, and a scrap of denim stuck to the bottom of the fence. The sky was lightening when Donna was satisfied that they had completely combed the area. They found a few good shoe prints in the woods a little beyond the treeline. The indentations were deep, as if the man who made them was carrying something heavy. When they sent the dog to follow the trail in the woods, it lost the scent at an access road, gravel-covered and too well traveled to collect tire prints. If he had carried the body to a vehicle to drive around the mountain and hike the shorter route up the hill to the mine shaft, somewhere there would be a vehicle with blood and forensic evidence in it.

They packed up for the trip back to Columbia, but Donna was thinking only of bed and a few hours of sleep.

He really should have been writing up the story of the county rezoning meeting, but his mind kept wandering back to Cher Anderson.

Carl Chambers had been a reporter for *The State*, the main daily paper serving Columbia. He was a good investigative reporter, but he always wanted something more. When the *McCormick Messenger* was looking for a new editor, he jumped on it. Even though it was a small town weekly paper, it was now *his* paper, and the only source of news for all of McCormick County.

He should have known going into it that the local people would have a hard time opening up to him—an outsider. He had been working for the last year to gain their trust, and the town folk seemed to be gradually warming up to him.

He fired up his computer and started a search on Cher. He learned that she was a rich divorcee and immediately thought "golddigger." He read on. Last spring she hosted the annual fundraiser for Juvenile Diabetes. The previous winter she opened her house for a Christmas tour to benefit the local libraries. Good grief! He was expecting to see next that she'd rescued kittens from a burning building. He looked back further.

She divorced her husband in 1984. Since Howard Anderson was wealthy and well connected, the story had made the news. There were claims of infidelity, and the gossip columns from that time named Howard's secretary, Dora Lakeland, as the other woman. Lakeland … he had just heard that name today. Cher said that the name of the accident victim's camping partner was Lakeland. He'd had a weird vibe when she mentioned him, like she was holding something back.

What Carl didn't find was any publishing credentials for Cher. He loved nothing more than solving a mystery, and Cher Anderson fit the bill.

"I never quite understood the attraction of grits," Cher said as they locked the motel room door. "They're pretty bland unless you drown them in butter, which would give them the fat content of hash browns cooked in the bacon grease left on the grill. What's the point?"

Cher was dressed in the business suit and silk blouse she had brought. The suit was a conservative gray with a pencil skirt and a well tailored jacket. Red sling-back pumps and a strand of pearls with matching earrings completed the ensemble.

They were startled by a voice from behind them. "Do you ladies know of any restaurants within walking distance? The continental breakfast here leaves a lot to be desired."

They turned to find Paul Lakeland walking from the direction of the motel office.

"I got kicked out of my campsite, and my friend's ride was impounded. I'm kind of stuck here for now."

"Why, we met you at Parsons Mountain Saturday." Cher said. "You told us where to find the mine shafts: that's where we found your friend."

"It was you who found him?"

Cher scrunched her forehead, as if searching her memory. "Your name is Paul, isn't it? There's nothing within walking distance, but we were just going out for breakfast if you'd like to join us. I'm writing a story of the murder for the local paper. Maybe you know something that can help us find the guy who did this. I'll spring for breakfast if you don't mind spitballing some ideas with us."

"I guess that would be okay. I didn't know Sam well, but I'd sure like to find out who did this."

They got in Maggie's jeep and drove to the inn.

Maggie was trying to figure out how they had gone from getting Cher her story to solving a murder. Had Cher mentioned it last night? By the time they had ordered breakfast, Maggie had come to the conclusion that they might just be able to pull off a murder investigation, all evidence to the contrary. The worst that could happen would be getting stumped and having to give it up. Cher was excited last night to have such an amazing story fall into her lap. If they could solve this murder, Cher's first byline could go national. She decided that it was the least she could do for her friend.

Maggie tried to remember the five "w's" of journalism: what, where, who, when, and why. "Let's start with why. Why did you guys come out here to camp?"

"I'm working on my doctoral thesis in Anthropology. We were checking out a possible Creek Indian burial site. Since Sam is … *was* my faculty advisor, he wanted to see the site before we applied for grants and permits to dig."

Cher was scribbling notes quietly, so Maggie continued. "One 'w' down. Where exactly was this site?"

"There's an entrance to an abandoned gold mine right next to our campsite. It's on the other side of the ridge from where we met, down at the base of the mountain. You have to go in the mine entrance to get access to the cave system."

"And your burial site is in the caves?"

"Yes. I found an urn my first time out here and took it to Sam to corroborate my find. He wanted me to keep it a secret until we had applied for the dig permit. He said that people would kill for less than an Indian burial ground." He shuddered and his hand started shaking as he took a sip of coffee. "I thought he was speaking figuratively. I didn't even know it was a murder, until the police picked me up last night. They asked the same questions we're talking about now, only then I felt like I was in the hotseat."

Cher gently touched his hand where it lay on the table. "You know, the police aren't happy unless they're making somebody uncomfortable."

"Okay," Maggie continued. "now the question is, could there be a connection between why you were at the mine, and why Sam was killed? Maybe you guys saw or heard something that seemed insignificant at the time, but would lead to our bad guy. If this were a movie, that would put you in danger and you wouldn't even know it. You'd be next on the list."

"Holy crap!" Cher shouted. The diners at the surrounding tables stared openly at her. "The news story about your car accident! What if somebody tampered with your car, and that's why the brakes failed?"

Paul went pale. "I had another accident last week. I fell off the balcony of my apartment. I don't usually drink much, but apparently I was snockered. I don't remember anything after Sam and I started toasting the discovery."

Cher was about to say something, when Maggie broke in.

"When? Something doesn't make sense here."

Cher glanced at her watch. "Maggs, look at the time. I have to go meet Mr. Chambers. Do you think we could get together for lunch and try to establish a timeline?" she asked Paul.

By now, Paul's hands were trembling enough that he had to put his coffee cup down.

"Do you really think someone might be trying to hurt me … to kill me?"

Just like that, Maggie's maternal instinct kicked in. "Why don't you stick close to me while Cher's at her meeting. Nobody's likely to try something if you're with somebody. Besides, I could use some help walking the dogs."

Paul's independent nature was battling with his sudden paranoia, and his fears won.

"You wouldn't mind having me tag along?"

"If you don't mind hanging out with a middle-aged lady and two hyperactive dogs."

"If you're right, it beats the alternative, besides, you're my ride."

Chapter Twenty-three

Cher picked her way across the railroad tracks and Main Street to meet with Carl Chambers at the *Messenger*. She inspected her new shoes to make sure she hadn't gouged the heels on the gravel from the tracks and checked her reflection in the window before entering. She looked immaculate and professional.

The front office of the *Messenger* looked old and a little tired. Dust floated in a sunbeam streaming through the window and there was a stale smell in the air. There were two sturdy wooden chairs pushed against the wall, and a vintage fan stood atop a filing cabinet. A wooden railing separated the front office from the back, where she could see a massive old mahogany desk with a leather swiveling chair. She loved it!

She had expected Carl to come out wearing an oxford shirt, unbuttoned at the collar and with the sleeves rolled up. Instead he had on another argyle sweater, the neck of his t-shirt showing above the v-neck. This one was orange and green, and made her think of Halloween. He ushered her through a gate in the railing. She ran her fingers along the top of the rail as she walked to the desk.

"Welcome to the *Messenger*, Cher. May I call you Cher? Feel free to call me Carl."

He pulled a wooden chair away from the wall and seated her across from him. His laptop, a lamp, and an old leather-bound blotter were the only occupants of the desktop. She was a little disappointed not to see an overflowing inbox and stacks of papers and files littering the dark chocolaty surface. She pulled out her laptop, asked for Carl's email address and within moments, she had sent in her first exclusive story. She watched intently as his eyes wandered across the screen.

Carl prided himself on taking things in stride, but he could literally feel his eyes bulge as he read the word "murder." He said nothing until he had finished the story, then he looked up at Cher.

"Not bad for your first story."

Cher straightened up and smiled. "Thank you!" Then it hit her that she had just tipped her hand.

"You kind of held out on me when you said that you were a journalist." Carl said mildly.

"I've taken journalism courses at the Community College and written some really fine stories for my classes." She rushed on, "I never claimed that I'd been published and I really didn't mean to mislead you. I just saw an opportunity that would be mutually beneficial for us."

"You broke one of the first rules of journalism, Missy. You failed to keep your editor in the loop."

Honestly, he couldn't count the number of times that he had gone Lone Ranger on a story. Fortunately, his editor at *The State* had gotten used to surprises.

"Why am I just now finding out that this has turned into a murder investigation?"

Cher blinked. "Well, I thought you wanted a finished story. I didn't want to turn in something half-baked."

"Where did you get your information?" Carl asked.

"From the Sheriff. When we went in for questioning yesterday evening, Officer Smith told us about the murder."

"You're telling me that Artie Smith gave you all these details?"

"To be honest, I think in the end he just wanted to get rid of me."

"Ho, ho, ho!" Carl crowed. "Cher, you are like kryptonite. Now I know his Achilles heel."

"Well, it was Sunday night and he was tired and hungry. I think I just caught him in a weak moment."

"Well done! I want to thank you for getting this story off to a good start. I need to do a little editing, but your article is good. I'll make sure you get the byline, but I'm afraid we're not set up to pay for stories."

"Then why not let me follow up on this. I think I could do a really good job for you."

He looked at her soberly. "Because you broke the second rule of journalism. Does the name Dora Lakeland mean anything to you?"

Cher paled.

"A journalist has to maintain objectivity, but you have a personal involvement in this story."

He waited, expecting her to explain her relationship with Dora Lakeland. When she remained silent, he continued kindly.

"You know that you're out of your league. An editor would never assign a murder story to a rookie reporter."

Cher looked up from the speck of dust that she'd been staring at. "Then the answer is 'no'? You won't even consider it?"

"Not unless you can solve a murder before the police do. Now that would be a breaking story! You have some talent, Cher, but you'll need more experience before you can handle the intricacies of a murder story. It's not as easy as it looks on TV."

Cher knew that he was being reasonable, but it did nothing to squelch the anger that was bubbling up. She had been ecstatic about getting this story. It was *hers*, and now it was being taken away. *"Not unless you can solve a murder before the police do,"* she thought. Hadn't she planned on doing that anyway?

"Fine." she said firmly as she closed her laptop and replaced it in her case. "Thank you for this opportunity, Mr. Chambers. I'll be in town a few more days if you need anything more from me." She handed him a card with her cell number, turned and left with as much dignity as she could muster.

Jonathan's office was on the second floor, a few doors down from *The Messenger*. He felt like a kid waiting for Santa Claus. He had dusted his leather bound legal books on the bookshelf behind his recently polished desk. His office was small, but well appointed. The sunshine streaming through the windows added a luster to the leather chairs and painted the oriental rug in rich crimson. He had just started the coffee pot when he heard a knock at the door. Before he could take two steps, Cher burst into the room, her cheeks flushed and her anger washing over the fine leather furnishings. She seemed to fill the office with her presence.

Jonathan had to grab the edge of the desk to stay on his feet. She was everything wild, and raw, and lovely. She stood trembling just inside the door as he walked over to her. Without a word, he ran the pad of his thumb in a whisper of a caress along her jaw. Her eyes focused on him and her lips parted.

Cher felt like she had just woken up from a dream as his lips found hers ... and she wanted more. She could barely breathe as his tongue gently traced the seam of her lips. She parted her lips further, tasting coffee, fresh fruit, and desire. She gasped as his hands unbuttoned her jacket and ran up her ribs, under her shell pink silk blouse, his fingers running along the bottom of her lace bra. Dear Lord, it had been so long since a man had touched her like that! She broke the kiss and was moving without thought, dropping her laptop onto a nearby chair, shrugging out of her jacket, and loosening his tie while his fingers continued their maddening brushes against her skin.

As if on cue, they broke, each fumbling with their shirt buttons. She tugged off his t-shirt, delighting in the light dusting of hair on his chest. He was kissing the swell of her breasts, and her fingers felt clumsy as she tried to undo his belt.

He kissed her again with an intensity that made her want to cry. He found the clip in her hair, and released the long blond tresses from her French roll, massaging the back of her neck with silken strands and steely fingers. He had backed her up to his desk, and now lifted her to sit on the edge. He ran his hands up her thighs, lifting her pencil skirt while gently parting her legs. She was exhilarated as he claimed her—his fingers marking her as his own.

She unfastened her bra and heard him groan as his fingers spread across her inner thighs. He watched, mesmerized as her generous breasts spilled out of her bra. She threw her head back and ran her fingers through his hair as his lips closed around one erect pink nipple.

There was a rushing noise in Cher's ears, so that she barely heard the click of the door. She looked over Jonathan's shoulder with eyes glazed by passion … just in time to see a wide-eyed Maggie, backing out the door so quickly that she ran right into Paul, who was standing in the hallway.

Maggie had never heard Cher swear before, but she clearly heard a squeaky, "Oh shit!" as she closed the door.

Maggie was completely at a loss for what to do. She shouted through the door, "We'll just be over at the Inn when you're, you know, done."

Cher looked apologetically at Jonathan and asked, "Rain check?"

"Ouch!" he replied as he straightened her skirt. "So, how do you take your coffee?"

Chapter Twenty-four

Maggie stood red-faced in the hallway. She could feel her ears burning. Paul didn't say a word for fully thirty seconds.

"Well, that was awkward. Maggie? C'mon, I'll buy you a cup of coffee."

In the office, Cher was no less embarrassed. She rushed over to get her blouse, clutching it to her chest as she stammered, I'm not usually, … I mean I don't, … I've never done anything like that in my life."

Jonathan picked up her bra from where it had fallen on the floor and handed it to her. He made a point of turning his back while he put his shirt back on. "So what do you want to know about me?"

Cher blinked, not sure that she had heard him right.

"I mean, the problem here is that we hardly know each other, ..." he turned to face her, "... and I would very much like there to be a *know* if we hit it off. You can't deny that we both felt a physical attraction."

"Jonathan, you've got to be twenty years younger than me."

"My full name is Jonathan Edward Miller, Esquire. I'm thirty-three years old, and a widower. I come from a poor family in a small town. I attended law school at Harvard and graduated in the top 10% of my class. I deal primarily in Estate and Probate legal representation. Your turn."

"I'm so sorry about your wife. How did she die? How long ago?"

"You should probably know that she was rich, and I wasn't." He said as he poured the coffee. "I was struggling to put myself through school when we met. We fell in love and got married within six months, and she used money from her trust fund to put me through law school. I was establishing my own practice when we decided to get pregnant. Before that could happen, there was a home invasion while I was at court. The thief must have been surprised to find her, because he only took some jewelry and her purse after he shot her. I found her myself when I got home later that afternoon. That was four years ago. People accused me of terrible things, and I was too numb with shock to try to defend myself. It was fodder for the gossip rags, but the police never charged me with anything. I have a practice and an apartment in Columbia, but this is my permanent residence. It's closer to my family, and farther from the media."

"Did they ever catch the man who did it?"

He stared into his coffee cup. "No."

He seemed to be lost in thought for a moment, so Cher merely waited.

"I tell you what, Cher, how about we have dinner tonight and we'll talk about you. I'm not the best cook, but I make a mean pot of chili."

"At your house?"

"Just the two of us. Does that scare you?"

She smiled softly. "I think I can behave myself."

Maggie knew that Cher was a grown woman, but she had never seen this kind of passion and abandon from her friend. She couldn't get the image out of her mind, so she tried for a neutral subject. "Why don't we talk about the murder while we're waiting for Cher? We know the location, so if it wasn't a crime of opportunity, there was some reason that he chose your camping site."

"I can't think why, unless he didn't know I was in the tent, and he thought this would be a secluded place. Fat lot of good it did to be there, since I didn't even wake up."

"You were lucky he didn't know, or you could be dead too…you could be dead."

Maggie was twisting her napkin around her finger, lost in thought. "What if it was the other way around? Maybe he didn't know Dr. Peters was there, and he thought he killed you."

"What do you mean?"

"Paul, you may be the only target. We assumed that he was after Dr. Peters, and might come for you next, but maybe he was trying to kill you all along. It's just as likely that he thought *you* were camping alone. Monday was the first attempt, so our missing piece of the puzzle happened before then."

"Last weekend is when I found the jar in the mine. I told Sam about it Monday morning."

"So you had never been there before last weekend?"

"No. There must be some mistake. Why would someone be coming after me?"

"If your brakes were tampered with, wouldn't there be some evidence of it?"

"My brakes..." Paul pulled out his cell phone and called his brother.

"Dan, have you finished working on my car? Do you know why the brakes failed?"

"I think Jimmy just finished it up." Dan said from the other end of the line. "I'll check with him and get back to you in a few."

"Thanks, Dan."

Cher walked in looking a little flushed. She sat down next to Maggie and fiddled with her fork.

"Well, what have you two been up to?" she asked.

Maggie smiled wickedly. "I don't have to ask you the same."

Cher put on a mock scowl. "We shall not speak of this again; at least not until after Jonathan and I have dinner tonight ... at his house."

"Ah, ha!" Whatever Maggie was about to say next was cut short by Paul's phone.

Paul's end of the conversation was cryptic with long pauses. "Hello? ... He did? ... They were? ... So what does that mean? ... Are you sure? ... Okay, thanks bro! ... I will."

"What did he say?" Maggie asked.

"The brakes themselves were just fine, but the brake fluid was gone. They checked the brake line and found two small holes. That would make some sense if the line was brittle and cracked, or if I'd been off-roading through gravel pits and threw up debris, but the line was in perfect condition other than the holes, and the undercarriage has a protective plate, so it's trail-rated. Dan thinks somebody cut the line intentionally."

"That's it!" Maggie said. "They *were* after you all along. Dr. Peters' death was just a terrible mistake. Cutting the brakes was meant to look like an accident."

Cher was already scribbling on her pad. "What are we talking about, Maggs? You think Dr. Peters wasn't the intended target?"

"That's exactly what I think, which casts doubt on the fall off the balcony being an accident as well."

Paul's face was white and sweat was forming on his upper lip. "I thought I'd just been having a really bad week."

"Nobody has that bad of a week?" Maggie declared. "Someone has to be following you to have tracked you down to such a remote location. Have you seen anything unusual this last week, maybe someone lurking about?"

"Lurking? Darling, that's downright cloak and dagger. I love it." Cher wrote the word in her note pad.

"I'm afraid I'm not too observant. I don't even notice when my shoes are untied."

Cher asked, "Do you have a regular pattern to your days? It's always easier to follow someone if they have a set routine."

"Well, I get to the lab on campus the same time every day. I'm generally the first one there."

"That's good," Cher said. "What time did your brakes go out?"

"It was in the morning. Each day after the interns arrive, I go out to my favorite coffee shop. I was on my way there when the brakes failed."

Maggie was thinking it through. "This was on Thursday—your birthday, Cher. First one there … first one. So your car was alone in the parking lot for awhile?"

"Actually, Sam's car was there in the faculty lot when I arrived, but it's the first time that I remember him being there before me."

"I wonder if there could be some connection."

"He was at my apartment Monday night too, when I fell off the balcony."

"That's it!" Maggie declared. "He must have been in on it."

Cher looked exasperated. "C'mon Maggs. Are you saying that the man faked his own death? It would be kind of hard to bludgeon yourself with a rock hammer. This isn't some Sherlock Holmes convoluted mystery."

Just then, Sheriff Smith walked into the inn. "Do you mind if I join you? I just have a couple questions for you, Paul."

"Okay."

Artie took the vacant seat at the table. It was against the wall so that he had a clean line of sight to the door. He took out his note pad. "You said last night that you were showing Dr. Peters a burial ground that you found?"

"That's right."

"And that this site would be your doctoral thesis project?"

"Yes."

"That would be quite a find, wouldn't it?"

"What are you getting at, sir?"

"This morning as we were searching Dr. Peters' office at the university, we found paperwork for grant requests and permits in his name."

"I asked him to help me with the paperwork."

"The papers pinpointed the exact location of the burial ground, with copies of aerial photos of the surrounding area. You said that he hadn't been to the site before this trip. You can see how that would make one think that you were trying to take the credit for Dr. Peters' find."

"But I *did* find it!" Paul insisted. "I've got the jar, the maps and aerial photos to prove it."

"Please stand up, turn around and place your hands behind your back." He said to Paul, "Paul Lakeland, I'm placing you under arrest for the murder of Samuel Peters. You have the right to remain silent."

"Paul didn't do it!" Cher said.

"Anything you say can and will be used against you in a court of law. You have the right to speak to an attorney and to have an attorney present during questioning."

"You're making a mistake, Sheriff …" Maggie blurted.

"If you cannot afford an attorney, one will be appointed to you."

"… Paul was the intended victim."

"Do you understand these rights as they have been read to you?"

Paul nodded in the affirmative and the Sheriff began to lead him out past curious diners.

"Paul, do you have a lawyer?" Cher called. "I can get you one."

"I'll be okay. Just tell them the jar is at my mom's house, and the research material is at my apartment. We can get this cleared up."

Cher was on the phone before the police car had pulled away from the curb. "Howard, this is Cher. We've got a problem. … It's Paul, Paul Lakeland. He's been arrested for murder. … He didn't do it, but that's not all. I think the murderer may have been after him and killed his friend by mistake, but now Paul's being charged with his friend's murder, and he's innocent. … Howard, I have *not* been drinking and this is not a joke. … I'll explain it later, right now do you know a good criminal lawyer? He's being held by the McCormick County sheriff's department. … Yes, I'm in McCormick now. If you can get him set up with a lawyer, I'll do what I can on this end. … Howard, he's your son, of course I want to help. … All right. Talk to you soon."

Cher closed her phone and looked helplessly at Maggie. "I'm not sure what to do now," she whispered.

"Well, for one thing, you'd better cancel your date."

Chapter Twenty-five

Maggie and Cher returned to the motel to gather up the dogs and search online for the address of Gene and Dora Lakeland.

"Cher, I swear you are a saint. How can you just walk up to that woman and offer to help her?"

"She can eat dirt, for all I care! But I like Paul, and it's not his fault that his x-chromosome comes from an idiot."

"You know, Sweetie," Maggie said, "there are a lot of very colorful terms for Dora Lakeland. Please feel free to reach into your forbidden lexicon at any time you feel the need this afternoon. I'll try not to go into shock if you swear."

Since they hadn't had a chance to eat lunch, they stopped at a gas station for chips and hot dogs. Fluffy and Buddy were far more appreciative of the latter.

"As God is my witness, I will never eat a gas station hot dog again!" Maggie exclaimed with a burp.

"I'll bet you a pack of Oscar Mayer wieners and a bag of buns."

"All beef, because those turkey dogs give me gas."

Cher laughed. "Okay, and we'll only make you hold out for one month, and just to show you I'm a good sport, I'll still bring my potato salad to the weenie roast when you lose."

"I'll bring my poppy seed cake when you lose. Maggie pulled back onto Highway 378, headed for Columbia. "Just so I know what to expect, what can you tell me about Dora?"

Cher looked thoughtful. "It's been such a long time since I saw her last. The woman is about as mean-spirited and vindictive as they come."

"What did Howard ever see in her?"

"She was pretty, just about the opposite of me. Dora had a tiny delicate figure, long black hair, and a mouth that would embarrass a sailor. For all her bluster, she was a very emotionally needy person. I guess she had a bad childhood or something. Maybe that's what drew Howard to her. He was attracted to someone hanging on his every word; someone who would cling to him like a lamprey on a shark; someone who would agree with everything he said and did. He always said he loved my independent spirit. Men are such idiots!"

"I'll bet she's still a little bitch," Maggie said. "Some things never change."

"I guess we'll find out soon enough."

Maggie had given up on her GPS shortly after it told her she was driving through a field. She didn't like the nagging voice on it anyway. Still, they were able to find the Lakeland home with a minimum of wrong turns. A row of nearly identical one story houses marred by neglect lined the street. Like most of the yards, the Lakelands' lawn consisted mostly of weeds and bare dirt. Paint was peeling from the wood siding, and the doors of the detached garage were hanging crookedly on the hinges. There was a chain-link fence around the yard, which was guarded by two pit bulls.

"Are you sure you want to do this, Cher? We could just walk away and let the police do their job."

"Do you see any police cars here? The police arrested the wrong man. You can't trust their objectivity when all their attention is focused on making a case against Paul. Besides, he's counting on us to help."

Maggie walked up to the gate and entered without hesitation. The dogs danced joyfully around her. They apparently didn't get many visitors. Even the frantic barking of Buddy and Fluffy in the car could not distract the pits from their new-found friend. Cher entered more tentatively, but the dogs were no less adoring of her.

"How did you know they wouldn't rip you apart?" Cher asked.

"I didn't, but I wasn't going to let them know that."

"I'll never understand you, darling. If these dogs were Chihuahuas wearing leggings, you'd be hyperventilating. Fair warning: if you're being attacked by anything with large teeth, don't expect me to come to your rescue. I love you, but I'm not keen on becoming part of the food chain."

It was Dora who answered the door. "If you're with the Jehovah's Witnesses, you can just keep your brochure."

Cher barely recognized her. Dora had been five foot six inches of delicate beauty. She had gained at least 40 pounds. Her face was round and puffy with dark circles under her eyes. Her jeans were straining at the seams and she had at least two inches of gray roots growing out of what was once a magnificent mane of ebony hair.

Maggie could see the moment that Dora's eyes lit with recognition.

"Cher Anderson, what a pleasure it is to see you again. You can see that I'm pretty busy, so I don't really have time to chat."

Dora was starting to close the door when Cher said simply, "Paul's in trouble. He needs your help."

Dora gave her a calculating look, then opened the door. "You have five minutes to explain what this is all about and why I should believe you."

They walked into a living room that was surprisingly tidy, except for the man sitting on the couch. He was heavy set, balding, and wearing blue boxer shorts and a white t-shirt, while he watched *The People's Court* on TV.

"Gene, can you turn that down? We've got company."

He barely looked up as he put his beer can on the coffee table and reached for the remote.

Dora led Maggie and Cher through the living room to the dining room where they sat at the table. She made no move to offer them coffee—no surprise. "The clock is ticking," she said.

"This is my friend, Maggie. We met Paul in McCormick a few days ago, when he gave us directions to a stream in the woods. He was camping with his faculty advisor, showing him a burial ground. His advisor was murdered there at the campsite and the police think that Paul did it. He asked me to find a jar he left here, and some documents in his apartment that will prove he's innocent. We think that somebody was trying to kill Paul, and got his advisor by mistake."

Cher expected Dora to ask how she knew Paul, why she wanted to help him, and why she thought he was the intended victim. What Dora said totally shocked her.

"How do I know you didn't do it?"

Maggie's jaw dropped. "Are you out of your mind?"

"Howard's been very generous to us over the years." Dora said. "He paid for this house and for Paul's college. He even set up a big fat trust fund for him. I didn't want Paul to know that he was a bastard, so I convinced Howard to support us anonymously, but you probably already know that. It must have eaten you up over the years, knowing that Howard's whore and bastard son were getting the money that you deserved. It would certainly give you a strong motive for murder: revenge. You kill Paul to get back at me, but you get the wrong guy. Oh, that would be rich!"

Cher stared at Dora, wide-eyed. She couldn't care less about Howard's financial support of Dora and Paul, but to have someone think she was capable of murder … she must have heard wrong.

"Don't worry," Dora continued, "I know you're too much of a puss to do anything like that. You gave up a good thing with Howard, just because of a little horsing around, then you didn't even ask for half of what you could have gotten in the divorce settlement, for crying out loud. No, you wouldn't want revenge, but I'm wondering what you *do* want."

Cher had rehearsed this explanation on the drive, but she was too bewildered to respond right away. How do you explain kindness to a self-centered evil harpy?

Chapter Twenty-six

"I want to make sure an innocent man, your son doesn't go to jail. Howard's already arranging for an attorney, but I promised Paul I would get the jar and the documents. They'll disprove the police's theory on a motive."

"Knock yourself out. His old room is down the hall, last door on the left. I have a copy of his apartment key. Do you need the address?"

"Yes, please."

Dora had that calculating look back in her eyes. "You know, if Paul's incarcerated, I guess I'll have to take over as executor of his trust fund. That would be a hoot."

Cher and Maggie walked down the hallway without another word.

Paul's room had obviously been turned into a junk room. There were old lampshades and boxes of newspapers on the bed. Two ten speed bicycles leaned against one wall, while stacks of boxes completely obscured the other wall from view.

"Dora apparently isn't the sentimental type," Maggie observed. "She's pretty much removed all evidence of Paul's existence. There's not even a poster on the wall."

Despite the mess, it didn't take them long to find the jar, wrapped in a sweater in the bottom of the closet.

"I'm just as glad we didn't have to look under the bed. We might have found his stash of porn," Maggie said.

"Or Gene's porn." They both cringed. "Paul's an archaeologist, so I half expected to find a mummy in the closet. If I had opened the door and seen one, I probably would have wet myself."

"Don't worry, Cher. If there had been a mummy, Dora would have long since sold it on eBay. We've got the jar, so time to find some research material."

Cher took one last look around the room. "I was afraid I'd feel like a voyeur, intruding on his life. Turns out there's little sign of life left in here."

As they reentered the dining room, they were stunned to see a young man standing just inside the kitchen: a very familiar looking young man.

"Oh, I didn't know we had company." He stepped into the dining room.

"But we know you," Maggie said. "You were hunting in the woods the other day when we were looking for gold mines. That was just before we found the body."

He scowled. "What body?"

"The man who was camping with Paul."

"Paul's my brother. I just talked to him a little while ago. He called about his jeep."

Maggie suddenly remembered. "Oh, you must be Dan. I was with him when he called you. That was just before they arrested him."

"*What*? He just asked me about his jeep. He never said anything about being arrested!"

"Right after your call, the McCormick County Sheriff arrested him for the murder of his faculty advisor, Dr. Peters," Cher said. "Paul asked us to help him by getting this jar and some research material from his apartment. We're going back out there to turn it over to the police."

"How will that help?"

"They think he was trying to steal Dr. Peters' research, when it was actually Paul's all along. His notes will prove that."

Just then, Dora walked in with the apartment key and a piece of paper.

"I'll tell you all about it, Dan."

"I think I've heard enough. I've got to get out there."

Without another word, Dan rushed out the kitchen door.

Dora looked at Cher. "Here's the key and his address. You know that if this evidence disappears, we'll have to assume that you're the murderer, but whichever one of you goes to jail, I win. I always win."

Cher had been scribbling notes in the car, and was still seething when they got to the apartment. "How can she be so callous about her own son? I tell you Maggs, if things go south, I will make sure to print every word in the news story. As I recall, she never said that she was speaking off the record."

"It is so cool having a reporter as a friend!"

They were able to find the research notes and photos right away.

"We'll need something to carry all this in. Can you find a box, or basket—something big?" Cher asked.

"Why haven't the police been here? Don't they normally get a warrant and search for evidence right away? This all just seems backwards somehow."

"Maggs, what if the police are in on this. They wasted no time finding evidence to incriminate Paul, and they don't seem too keen on looking any further."

"Okay, Cher, you just gave me the creeps. I'd say that's an outrageous conspiracy theory if I didn't half believe it."

They gathered up maps and photos, and found four spiral bound notebooks that were filled with what looked like thesis notes. Maggie found several cloth shopping bags under the sink, which they loaded up for the trip back to McCormick.

They let the dogs run around in the park across the street for a few minutes while they had a cigarette.

Cher took a long thoughtful drag. "You know, darling, I just think it's odd that Dan was hunting in the exact area where the body was found, and his dogs didn't pick up on it like ours did."

"Or they did just before we got there, but he already knew the body was there. Cain and Abel—jealousy is the oldest motive in the book. Paul has a trust fund and Dan apparently doesn't. If Dan came to McCormick the night before the hunt, he was in the right place at the right time. You know, Cher, Dan is a mechanic. He would know how to cut brake lines. He comes and goes at his mom's house, so he would also have access to this key, the one to Paul's apartment. He looks strong enough to easily throw someone off a balcony."

Cher sighed. "I guess I'd better call Howard and find out who benefits from that trust fund if Paul dies."

They were lost in their own thoughts on the drive back to McCormick. Maggie tried to imagine Cher committing a murder. She had known her for six years, so that story didn't wash. Still, Cher had been distraught and a little drunk the night of the murder, and had disappeared from the room for some indeterminate period of time. Maggie shuddered. No way could Cher have dragged a fully grown man's dead weight up a steep hill and dropped him into a pit, … unless she had help.

"Howard, did you create a trust fund for Paul?" Cher asked.

"Why do you want to know?"

Cher scowled at the phone. Just hearing his voice rattled her. "Listen, I'm not upset that you've been supporting Paul all these years. I'm proud of you for being responsible about it. I just need to know who would benefit from Paul's death, and who would be executor of the trust if Paul goes to jail. It goes to motive."

"You'll have to talk to Paul's lawyer about that. I'm not going to hand you any information that might incriminate Paul."

"Oh, for Pete's sake, Howard! I'm trying to help Paul by finding his murderer. I mean we believe that Paul was the intended victim, and the murderer is still out there. If we can establish a motive, it can help us track down the real murderer, and Paul will be set free."

"Cher, I absolutely forbid you to pull some hair-brained stunt. You're not Nancy Drew, and I won't have you putting yourself in danger, not even for Paul. Let the police handle it."

"You forbid me? Really? You can't tell me what to do, Howard! And as for the police, they're already convinced that Paul did it. They're more concerned with building a case against him than investigating other avenues. You can't stop me, Howard, so you may as well help me. If not, I'll have my lawyer get an injunction ... or whatever the hell that form is!"

"Just try it!"

"Good-bye, Howard." Her words rang with finality.

Chapter Twenty-seven

Artie Smith had left the Special Forces with skills that would have qualified him for law enforcement just about anywhere, and he would rather be just about anywhere. He had settled in McCormick so that Carla could be closer to her family. Fifteen years of marriage, and she was still the same beautiful girl who had walked down the aisle. He didn't get along particularly well with her family. They were crude and resentful of Carla, for what they deemed her success. They should have been happy for her: she had a good education and a loving marriage. Why she wanted to live near them was anybody's guess. Worst of all, she insisted that he be nice to them, even when they made cruel remarks about her.

At least her brother, Andy, defended her when the others said hurtful things. He and Andy did some hunting and fishing together, and he was the only one of the lot of them who ever had anything interesting to say. Andy had worked hard to get where he was today. That was more than he could say for the rest of the family.

This murder investigation was the only exciting thing that had ever happened during Artie's tenure in this backwater town, and even it was open and shut. It had all been just too easy for his satisfaction. The suspect practically dropped the murder weapon in his lap. He had established motive and opportunity in the case against Lakeland.

It had been a long day, with a trip to Dr. Peters' office at the University and all the paperwork for the arrest. His mind started to drift. Sometimes he dreamed of finding the motherlode in one of the old mines and running away with Carla to Paris or Fiji.

He looked up as Mike walked into his office.

"Got the preliminary report here from the crime scene folks in Columbia."

Artie took the folder from him, and opened to the front page ... and sighed. There was a picture of a footprint from a trail near the crime scene with a ruler next to it. The shoe was size 11. He reached for the file in his drawer and examined the inventory of personal effects taken from Paul Lakeland when he was booked six hours ago. Men's hiking boots, size 9. He made a note to call the morgue and find out what size shoes the victim wore.

The size 11's had left a deep enough depression to suggest that the wearer was either overweight or carrying something heavy. They were consistent in tread pattern to any number of brands of hunting boots on the market. Well, there were hunters crawling all over these hills, and there was no way to be sure whether the wearer was carrying a hog carcass or a man. He also couldn't rule out the possibility that Lakeland had help.

He had sent Paul's clothes and shoes to the lab. Blood spatter was found around and on the camping table, there was even some on the tent, but nothing showed up on Lakeland's clothes or shoes. Proving his case would be a little more of a challenge, but he was up to the task.

Mike was waiting expectantly, frankly curious, but he excused himself when the phone rang.

"Sheriff Smith," Artie answered. He listened for a long time to the woman. When she identified herself as Dora Lakeland, he had expected a plea of her son's innocence. Instead, he was regaled with the story of an affair 26 years ago, and the part that Cheryl Anderson played in the love triangle. He listened patiently, taking careful notes before asking, "Why are you telling me this?"

"That woman would do anything to get back at me. So you think it's a coincidence that she just shows up on my doorstep today, looking for evidence to prove Paul's innocence?"

"She did what?" Artie nearly shouted.

"I was so beside myself with worry for Paul that I let her search his room and his apartment. Now I'm starting to have second thoughts. I don't trust her, Sheriff. She never tried to contact Paul or me for 26 years, but as soon as my boy gets in trouble, she's right in the middle of it. She could just as easily be trying to prove his guilt. You should also know, that Howard set up a very generous trust fund for Paul. He supported Paul and me for years, and paid Paul's college tuition and expenses. It makes you wonder about how the money was reported in Howard's finances. Did Cher know about this additional money all these years? Honestly, I don't know what to make of this, but it sure sounds fishy."

"You can be sure that I'll be talking to Ms. Anderson very soon. May I get your number in case I have any questions for you?"

Artie wrote down the number, thanked her, then hung up.

From an open and shut case, he suddenly had an embarrassment of riches: multiple suspects and motives;

possible accomplices; an attempted frame-up. He took out a fresh notepad and started a list.

It was a little after 6:00 PM when they arrived back at the motel. Maggie had spent the drive wondering how well she really knew her friend. She had never found it odd that Cher rarely spoke about her marriage. She had been divorced for almost 20 years when they met six years ago; by then it was old news. Cher was a beautiful, intelligent, vibrant woman, but until recently, she wasn't mysterious. What else was she hiding, and why?

In the last few days she had been faced with a painful chapter from her past, had shown an uncharacteristic ambitious nature where her writing was concerned, and had wasted no time getting better acquainted with her lawyer. That last one had thrown Maggie for a loop.

Maggie wondered how she would have reacted if her past had come crashing in on her. Her family would probably want to keep her away from the good china, or any other breakables. She still regretted having only seven dinner plates left in a pattern that was now discontinued. Throwing plate number eight had felt good at the time.

She just didn't want to see Cher get hurt, and she would have words with Jonathan to that effect as soon as she saw him again.

"Before we take Paul's records and jar to the police, let's get our facts straight, darling." Cher said as she booted up her laptop. "Item one: we both agree that Paul was likely the intended victim. Item two: the murder attempts have been confined to this last week, so there must have been something very recent that triggered the killer's motivation."

Maggie studied her shoes as she thought. "Maybe it has something to do with finding this jar in the first place. Wasn't it just last weekend when Paul found it in the cave?"

"Yes, then he showed it to his faculty advisor—now deceased—who started paperwork for an archaeological dig. I really think the whole 'stealing the discovery' nonsense has nothing to do with the murder, Maggs. I think we need to look at the location."

"Cher, you're a genius! The troubles all begin and end in McCormick, at that mine. Is somebody trying to hide something in the mine and Paul got too close? You know what I'm thinking?"

"Rarely."

Maggie gave a sly wink. "I'm thinking field trip. We only have one flashlight, since you dropped yours in the pit. I'm sure that they'll have flashlights at the gas station. We can get some more of their crummy hot dogs to eat on the way."

"Maggie, I think you've lost it. You're suggesting we tromp around the woods in the dark looking for a mine that we've never been to?"

"When we were at the police station, I overheard an officer talking about an access road near the ditch we panned in. It's supposed to lead to the mine. They said that they needed to open it up so forensics could get in there. How much you want to bet it's still open?"

Cher looked dubious.

"Look, if we don't find the road, we'll follow the trail to the mine tomorrow morning. Are you in?"

"That depends, darling. Are you buying the hot dogs?"

Chapter Twenty-eight

"Easiest bet I ever won," Cher said before taking her last bite of the hot dog.

"Yeah, but I'm still holding you to the potato salad."

"Do you think this is the stupidest thing we've ever done?" Cher asked.

"I'd say it's right up in the top two. But just think, if we can find the real motive for the murder, we may even be able to solve this crazy thing. Paul will be free, you'll have your story, and I'll have something really interesting to talk about with my therapist. Everybody wins."

"Except for the murderer. That's the part I don't like, Maggs. We're going to a place where a cold-blooded killer crushed another man's skull. What if he's still nearby?"

"These guys always have to lay low after the crime. It's the perfect time for us to slip in and see what all the fuss is about."

The last rays of sunshine were painting the treetops when they reached Parsons Mountain. There was still enough light so they had no trouble finding the access road to the mine. They parked the jeep next to the mine entrance and let the dogs out. There was little left of the campground, other than some crime scene tape. They gathered the flashlights and gave the dogs a few minutes to run before squeezing through the gap between the chain link fence and the rock wall at the mine entrance.

"Somewhere in here is the reason that Dr. Peters died, I'm sure of it!" Maggie whispered.

"I think it's pretty safe to say that we're alone, darling. You don't really need to whisper."

Cher had a point. The dogs were jumping around, their panting echoing down the mineshaft like the hissing of a flock of angry geese. They passed a corridor leading off to the right, but decided to keep going straight, for no better reason than that going straight would minimize their chances of getting turned around and losing their way. They continued what felt like about a quarter of a mile when Maggie stopped abruptly. "Do you hear water?"

Cher listened carefully. "It sounds like we're getting closer to it, but we're not moving. That means the water's coming closer to us." She paled. "I've heard of flash floods in these old mines."

There was a sudden change in air pressure preceding a torrent of black pouring out of a fissure in the mine wall. The air was alive with thousands of bats. The beating of their wings created a deafening roar echoing through the corridor. Maggie and Cher dropped face first to the ground with a collective screech, their hands covering their heads. Fluffy was in a panic and Buddy was jumping up and down trying to catch some of the elusive creatures. Not even the imminent danger of being trampled by the excited dogs could budge the girls from their protective positions. Just as quickly, the flood of bats was gone.

"It's dusk: they're going out to feed." Maggie said, her voice muffled with her face still pressed into the dirt. "I think we found the cave."

"D'ya think?"

Maggie stood up, so Cher followed suit.

"What do you say, should we go in the cave, or stay in the mine?" Maggie asked.

"If Paul doesn't know he stumbled onto something and he went in the cave, I vote that we explore farther into the mine. He may have just gotten too close to something down there."

Maggie looked around and was dismayed to find that Fluffy had gone AWOL. She shone her flashlight on the floor, looking for a clue of which way the cowardly mutt had gone. A little beyond the cave entrance, she found what she was looking for, and then some. Next to the scuffed paw prints of a dog running blindly deeper into a dark mineshaft were the footprints of men. Maggie turned a corner and found a very modern lantern hanging on one of the supporting beams.

"This is where the smoking pays off," Maggie said, as she pulled a lighter out of her pocket. The lantern light flooded the passageway, so they turned off their flashlights. Maggie called for Fluffy, her voice echoing eerily. She heard whining further down the mineshaft, but hadn't taken ten steps in that direction before she felt the walls reverberating with a rattling sound.

Maggie could feel beads of sweat on her upper lip. "Snakes. It sounds like the corridor is full of them. Fluffy is down there in a nest of rattlesnakes! Cher, stay here with Buddy."

"You're not going down there with a tunnel full of snakes! Fluffy! Come here, boy."

"I can't leave him down there. You take the flashlights and wait here. I'll be in and out in a minute."

Maggie hurried down the mineshaft, watching the ground carefully. She reached a chamber at the end without seeing any snakes. The rattling stopped, and she held her lantern high. She was in a chamber about thirty by thirty feet with a low ceiling. A wheelbarrow stood next to a large pile of rock and dirt in one corner of the room. Two pick axes and a shovel were propped up in another corner. There was no sign of Fluffy, but she heard a soft whimpering from a dark hole in the wall to her left. She carefully approached, and as her light ate through the dark of the crevice, she saw Fluffy curled up and shaking on the floor. It was little more than an alcove, but the back wall was shining brightly with a horizontal stripe of sparkling white and amber colored crystals. It took her a few moments to realize that the amber color was actually the reflection of gold in the crystals.

She bent down to comfort Fluffy, whose eyes shone with reflected light and adoration. Maggie took Fluffy's collar to urge him to stand up, then hurried back up the corridor to Cher. As she approached, the rattling began again. She quickly scanned around her feet, before lifting her lantern high. She saw a black box attached to the crossbeam of the support timbers. She followed the wires, tacked along the back side of the beam to a small speaker at ground level. "It's a motion sensor, and the rattling is just a recording."

"Are you sure, Maggs?"

Maggie beckoned Cher past the black box, and within seconds, the rattling stopped.

"Cher, I found the 'something' we were looking for! Somebody has been digging down here, and they struck gold."

They hurried back to the mine chamber, where Cher took the lantern and stepped inside the crevice. She whistled softly. "Somebody was willing to kill a man to keep this a secret. Maggie, we are in deep doo-doo. If anybody comes down here, there's no way we can get past them without being seen."

Maggie felt the hair on the back of her neck stand on end. Without a word, they hurried up the mineshaft, past the motion sensor, past the cave entrance, past the intersecting corridor and out to the chain link fence. Nobody there.

Maggie realized belatedly that she still held the lantern. There was no way she was going back in there to return it to the place where she found it. They loaded the dogs and extinguished the lantern, which Maggie hid behind a large rock near the entrance.

Cher was in the jeep, her heart pounding so hard that she could hear the rush of her blood pumping. Maggie's hands were white on the steering wheel and Cher was sitting on the edge of her seat, clutching the dashboard as they watched the headlights illuminating trees and bushes along the narrow access road.

Maggie felt a pain in her chest. *Not now. Please, not now.*

Not until they had left the forest service roads, and turned onto highway 29, did Maggie's breathing start to slow down. You can only stay in a state of panic for so long, and she was sure that the last twenty minutes had exhausted her supply of adrenaline.

Paul had waived his right to an attorney during the interrogation. He repeatedly claimed that he was the intended victim: hardly the defense that Artie had expected.

The incident reports he'd requested for the fall from the balcony and failed brakes had just arrived by fax. He wasn't willing to bet the farm that three close encounters with death were all a coincidence. If Paul was the intended victim, he could think of two possible motives: revenge and greed. Cher Anderson was the prime suspect for the former, and the beneficiary of Paul's trust fund was the candidate for the latter. He'd have to get a warrant to get a look at Cher's financial records. She wasn't strong enough to carry a body up a mountain and throw him into a pit, but if he could find a large withdrawal recently, she could be behind a murder for hire.

There was also the possibility that the murderer killed Dr. Peters on purpose, with the intent of framing Paul for the crime. Again, the same motives came into play. Who would be executor of the trust fund if Paul were in prison?

The motive he had assigned to Paul of stealing the credit for the find was looking weaker by the minute. *Dammit!* This was no time to be second guessing himself. Paul said that he had taken his jeep to one of Andy's garages, where they found that the brake lines had been cut. That would be easy enough to verify.

That bootprint was still the fly in the ointment. Mr. Size 11 was either acting on his own, working with one of the suspects, or a random hunter, totally unrelated to the murder. Artie's moral compass wouldn't allow him to blindly continue to build a case against Paul just to get a conviction on his record. Someone in this town was a murderer, and he was determined to find out the truth.

He changed mental gears and pulled out the forensics report and the coroner's report, ready to read them again based on the assumption that Paul was the intended victim.

Chapter Twenty-nine

Cher's hands were shaking slightly as she lit a cigarette. The lighter flipped out of her sweaty fingers and rolled under the car seat. "What now? It could be anyone in this town. They all seem to know about the abandoned mines, so every last one of them from the garbage man to the Mayor could have wandered in there and found the gold."

"Let's not forget, Cher, we have hunters like Dan coming in from all over the area … with really big guns. I think I've read too many Stephen King novels with creepy small towns. Sometimes, everybody's in on it, or it's the friendly local policeman who ends up hacking the characters into little tiny bits. Please tell me I'm just being paranoid."

"I wish I could. Someone in town committed murder to keep this place a secret. If we tell the wrong person what we know, we'll be placing ourselves in danger. As it is, the killer is going to find the lantern missing and know that somebody's been down there." Cher's gaze dropped to her feet. "Oh sugar! I'm wearing heels. If I left any footprints, they're going to be girlie looking."

Maggie hissed, "Stupid, stupid, stupid. What the hell was I thinking? Cher, I'm sorry I got us into this. Between my holding onto the lantern and your comfortable yet stylish footwear, we may as well have left a sign with our motel room and cell phone numbers. We've got to get away from here."

"But the Sheriff asked us to stay. If we take off now, it's just going to make us look more suspicious."

Maggie was drumming her fingers on the steering wheel. "It's not going to take long to figure out it was us in the mine. As long as we're the only ones to know about the gold, all the killer has to do is get rid of us to keep his secret. If everybody knows about the mine, there's no more reason to kill us."

"I can think of a few, but I'm open to suggestions."

"In the movies, if the heroes think the police are in on it, they go to the news."

"Brilliant, darling! I *am* the news! I'll write everything up and get it to Carl in the morning. We haven't exactly solved the murder, but I don't think he'd pass up a story like this."

"Cher, any newspaper would kill for this story!" Maggie immediately regretted her choice of words. " … figuratively speaking."

When they returned to the motel, Maggie made a loop through the parking lot, scanning for any sinister looking cars with tinted windows. They glanced back over their shoulders repeatedly while walking the dogs, then hastily retreated into the motel room. They had a ration of microwave popcorn in the room, but neither of them had an appetite. Cher went right to work on her story while Maggie fed the dogs.

Gold vein possible motive for murder

Recent findings suggest that the motive for Saturday night's homicide in the Parson's Mountain area was to hide a covert mining operation. When this reporter investigated the scene of the crime, she found that there was a vein of gold exposed deep in the old mine, with evidence of recent activity. In addition, a motion sensor was found in the mineshaft. When the sensor was tripped, a speaker produced a loud rattling noise, easily mistaken for rattlesnakes in the mine. This was believed to be put in place as a deterrent to anyone who wandered into the shaft.

Police have arrested Paul Lakeland for the murder of his colleague, Dr. Samuel Peters. The two were camping together at the mouth of the mineshaft at the time that Dr. Peters was bludgeoned to death with a rock hammer. It is believed that the murder took place at their campsite, then the body was dumped into one of the old mine pits on the western side of the mountain ridge.

During the week preceding the murder two separate incidents now appear to be attempts against Mr. Lakeland's life. While a fall from his fifth story balcony Monday night cannot be deemed positively as foul play, it becomes suspect in light of a traffic accident Thursday, which was found to be the result of cut brake lines on Lakeland's car. This suggests that the murder of Dr. Peter's may

> have been a third failed attempt against Lakeland.
>
> Dr. Peters and Mr. Lakeland were conducting a reconnaissance of a possible Native American burial ground for the University of South Carolina's Anthropology Department. The site had to be accessed through a cave entrance a quarter of a mile into the shaft of the old Parson's Mountain gold mine. The site was discovered by Mr. Lakeland the Saturday preceding the murder.
>
> The timing of the burial ground discovery, the attempts on Lakeland's life, and the murder of Dr. Peters would suggest that Lakeland's exploration of the mine area the prior Saturday did not go unnoticed.

Cher was satisfied that her article had all the W's covered. By tomorrow morning, for better or worse, the secret would be out. Depending on how many people were in on this, they would either be safe, or the guests of honor at a town lynching.

Even with the comfort of Fluffy's warm back pressed against her side all night, Maggie got very little sleep. Her mind was racing, and she started at every sound. Who knew the flushing of a toilet in the room next door could take on a sinister quality?

She was grateful when the first rays of sunlight shone through a crack in the blackout curtains. Cher was still sleeping, and it was way too early to go get breakfast. As soon as she stepped out of the bathroom, she found Buddy and Fluffy looking anxiously at the door. *Hell!* She dressed and picked up the dogs' leashes, which sent them into a frenzy. She peeked through the curtains, saddled up the dogs, and gathered her courage to open the door. The hail of gunfire that she expected to walk into did not materialize.

By the time she got back to the room, Cher had woken up and was in the bathroom. Maggie set up the two-cup excuse for a coffee pot while Cher showered. After Maggie took her turn in the shower, they shared the bathroom for fluffing and foofing their hair. Maggie didn't wear make-up as a rule, but she wanted to have mascara on, just in case the worst happened. She didn't want to dwell on what "the worst" could be, but she was damned well going to look good for it.

They still had time to kill before it would be a decent hour for breakfast, and they were just as glad to hide out in the room until then. They smoked, drank their coffee, and played two rounds of cribbage.

"I don't think I'll feel safe until this story is out," Cher said. "Do you think that we should also contact a local radio or TV station? The *Messenger* is a weekly paper, and I'm not sure when the next issue comes out. I honestly don't know if I can keep up this level of panic that long."

"We'll ask Carl about it this morning and decide from there. He'll have better connections with other news sources, so he's equipped to help us get the word out. Remind me to call Ted today so he doesn't start worrying. I don't think I have the nerve to tell him that we were playing junior detectives and got ourselves in a pickle."

"You're going to lie to Ted?"

"Withholding information is a totally different thing. Besides, after we talk to Carl the immediate danger will be over. I'd rather not be hysterical when I talk to Ted."

"This is ridiculous," Cher exclaimed. "We can't hide out in the room forever. Let's take the dogs for a walk and let them run off some energy. By the time we're done, the inn will be open for breakfast."

"Are you delirious? Are the benefits of fresh air and exercise worth your life? If we go out in the open, we're just setting ourselves up as easy targets for a drive-by shooting or a hit and run 'accident'!"

"Listen, as long as we're shut up here, we're sitting ducks. If we're out and moving around, we'll be harder to find."

Maggie wasn't sure she agreed with the program, but she had lost both hands of cribbage, and was ready to do anything, even exercise, to take her mind off possible bludgeoning. A walk in the park would be the least of her problems.

Chapter Thirty

After their walk, the girls were happy to be at the inn. It was a nice public place with lots of witnesses, and they were both keenly aware that they had missed dinner last night. They had Paul's jar and notes hidden in the closet of their room, a terrifying secret until they could verify that the police weren't in on the murder.

From their table, they could see across the street, so they'd know when Carl arrived at the *Messenger*. They wanted to get Cher's article to him as soon as he opened up for the day. The food had just arrived when Sheriff Smith walked into the inn and came straight to their table.

Without preamble he said, "Ms. Anderson, I'll need you to come to the station with me to answer a few questions."

Maggie shot Cher a panicked look. Her friend looked pale and her eyes had dilated, leaving only a thin ring of blue around the pupil.

"Are you arresting her?" Maggie asked quietly. "You don't have to go, Cher."

"Ms. Anderson, we could do this the hard way if you prefer."

Maggie choked. Had he watched too many episodes of *Law and Order?* She placed her hand on Cher's, which felt no less clammy than her own. She glared at the Sheriff, then turned to Cher. "Honey, I'll get Jonathan. You don't have to answer anything until he gets there."

"You owe me some carrot cake, darling, and be sure to bake a file in it." Cher gathered some toast in a napkin and rose to leave.

As soon as Cher was out the door, Maggie flagged over the waitress, handed her a twenty and rushed outside. She watched the police car pulling away with her friend, then hurried across the railroad tracks and Main street to Jonathan's office. She took the stairs two at a time and was relieved when she found the door unlocked.

Jonathan turned from pouring his coffee as she burst in. "Maggie! Is there something wrong?"

"The police have taken Cher for questioning! You need to get over there before she cracks."

"Whoa! Why is she being questioned?"

"The Sheriff didn't say. You just need to get over there, while I go to the motel for the evidence."

Jonathan blanched. "What evidence?"

"Paul's jar and research notes. It will prove that he wasn't trying to steal the dig away from Dr. Peters. If the police know about it and think that Cher's holding something back, it will look bad for her."

"Where did you get this?"

"We went to his mom's house and his apartment yesterday."

"You gathered evidence … in a murder investigation … to take to the police? Maggie, have you no clue about the chain of evidence? I'll have to go with you to get the jar. If a disinterested third party brings it in, we might be able to salvage some credibility for it."

"But, Cher …"

"She'll be all right, Maggie. You're staying at the Sleepytime Motel? It will only take us a few minutes to get the jar and get back to the police station."

Maggie was trembling when they got to the jeep.

"We've got to hurry. Who knows what they're doing to her? The Sheriff may be in on it." She was rambling and she knew it. She just needed to make Jonathan understand the urgency.

"In on what?"

"The gold at the old mine. We found it last night, and until we can get Cher's story to the press, we're the next likely victims. Right now, we know too much."

"Cher wrote a story about gold at the mine? The Parsons Mountain mine? Where's this story?"

"It's in Cher's laptop, in the back. I've got to get it to Carl at *The Messenger* as soon as I drop you at the police station."

They had pulled up to the motel room. Maggie hadn't taken the time to make a loop of the parking lot. She just wanted to get the evidence and get out of there. She and Jonathan were both looking around carefully as they stepped out of the jeep. She turned to put her key card in the door.

An hour and a half had passed and still no Maggie. Maybe she had trouble tracking down Jonathan. Cher was glad she brought the toast with her, because it turns out that interrogations were rather boring. She had been sitting in a small room with a styrofoam cup of really bad coffee while waiting for her lawyer. She wasn't sure what she had expected when they put her in the room, but her state of terror had passed about half an hour into her solitary wait. Now she was just getting annoyed. She looked at her watch for the third time in the last five minutes. *"Damn!"*

They had locked the door from the outside, so she had little to do but wait. She looked at her watch again. That was enough, she was done waiting. She knocked on the door to the room, and a tall black man opened the door. Cher recognized him as one of the officers at the mine when they recovered Dr. Peters' body. "Excuse me, your name is Mike, isn't it?"

He nodded.

Time to turn on the charm. "They took my cell phone, Mike. I need to make a call."

"I'm sorry, ma'am. I can't let you do that."

Okay, charm wasn't working. "Nobody has read me my rights, so I haven't been arrested. You can't keep me locked up here against my will and you have no right to confiscate my phone. If you plan on arresting me, I'm still allowed one phone call. I need to call my friend and see what the holdup is."

"I'll ask the Sheriff, ma'am." He turned and closed the door.

A moment later the sheriff entered with another cup of coffee. I'm sorry for the delay. I brought you some more coffee if you'd like."

"What I'd *like* is to call my friend and see what's taking so long."

"Be my guest."

Artie pulled her phone from his shirt pocket and handed it to Cher. She tried Maggie's number … no answer. She pulled Jonathan's card out of her purse and tried his number … no answer.

Fear for her friend felt like it was eating a hole in her stomach. Cher was desperate to find somebody she could trust. She flashed to Stephen King and friendly small town police. This wasn't a novel, it was real life, and Cher was running out of options. She decided to take her chances.

She turned to Artie. "Let's talk."

Chapter Thirty-one

Something was making her light-headed and a little queasy … gasoline? No, it reminded her of camping as a kid … a kerosene lantern. She was drifting off again, and her head was throbbing. She remembered being with Jonathan…opening the door to the motel. Wait, did she actually open the door?

Her eyes flew open, but there was nothing to see. Maggie blinked twice, three times to make sure that her eyes truly were open, but all she saw was black. She felt like she was floating in it, but she could feel the hard ground under her. It helped to clear the confusion and keep her from drifting off into that deeper darkness again. That kerosene smell was not going away, and now she could fairly taste it. It felt like it was burning her lips and nose, causing bile to rise up in her throat. She tried to open her mouth, but there was something covering it. That was the source of the smell.

Easily fixed: just reach up and move it out of the way. The first shrug of her shoulders brought a stabbing pain to her neck, followed by a steady ache. The throbbing in her head was maddening. She was lying on her side, her hands bound behind her back, and her ankles tied together. The gag was apparently used to wipe kerosene spills, probably from lanterns, like the one she had found in the mine.

She was in the mine? Panic threatened to short out all her senses. She didn't have time for this. Time. How long had she been out? What happened to Jonathan? Had they gotten him too? Jonathan …

Oh dear God! She had blabbed everything to him on the drive to the motel. He knew that they had found the gold. He knew about the newspaper story, and that they hadn't gotten it to Carl yet. He was the *only* one who knew it all.

If he went back to the police station after dropping her here, he could be getting Cher released right now. She would trust him over the police. Hell, they had been scrumping like bunnies. Of course Cher would tell him everything before she would talk to the police.

Jonathan could return at any moment. For that matter, he could be standing right next to her and she wouldn't know it in the dark. She strained to hear breathing, scuffing feet on the floor, or maniacal laughter. There was nothing. She thought of Ted and stifled a sob. Would she ever see him again? What would Sally say about her predicament? She waited for the incredible pain in her chest and shortness of breath, but it never came. Maggie finally had a good reason for a panic attack and she wasn't having one. Would that qualify as irony?

She rubbed the side of her face against the ground, trying to work the odious rag off over her chin, and away from her mouth and nose. She managed to get it pulled down with a minimum of scraping to her cheek. She started wriggling about, feeling around on the ground behind her for anything sharp she could use on the ropes.

Her left shoulder was held together with pins and screws after a nasty fracture two years ago. Her right shoulder was prone to muscle spasms resulting from pinched nerves. Her past injuries combined with the unnatural constriction of her arms sent out shocking pain, especially when she tried to reach farther behind herself to search the ground. Hell, she broke a sweat when she had to open a new jar of peanut butter.

After wriggling what felt like the length of a football field, but couldn't have been more than ten feet, her hand brushed up against a rock. It was small, but the edge was jagged. She twisted her hand to start sawing at the unforgiving rope. Geez, Jonathan couldn't have used something softer to tie her hands? She cringed just to think his name, and nearly dropped the rock.

Suddenly she was giggling. She couldn't help it. Here she was facing imminent death, and all she could think about was the poor quality of her bindings? It was a huge relief to laugh, but she knew that he could be nearby, and she wouldn't know it. She didn't need to advertise that she was awake. Just then, she felt a give in the rope, and started sawing with renewed purpose. If he wanted to kill her, she wasn't going to make it easy for him.

As long as Cher was afraid to tell the police about the mine, he had a chance. Get rid of Maggie and the laptop, and he could deal with Cher later. He'd left Maggie in the abandoned dig site at the end of the north shaft. They had been using it to store their gear, since it was higher ground, with less chance of flooding if it rained. The river in the cave could overflow its banks and become a raging torrent in a good rainstorm, backing up into the mineshaft. He and Andy had had to wear their waders to dig during one particularly bad storm. He would just hurry down to the dig, grab one of the pick axes, and dispatch Maggie the same way he had that Peters fellow. As he reached the main shaft, he saw the glow of a lantern coming from the mine entrance. He heard Andy call out, "Who's down there?"

"Just me, Andy."

As he approached Jonathan, Andy asked, "Ya get a new car, Bear? Nice lookin' Jeep."

"Nah, it's a loaner. My truck wouldn't start this morning."

"You're dressed up pretty spiffy for diggin'."

"Gus said he saw some kids playing around the entrance while he was out hunting yesterday. I'm meeting a client this afternoon, but I just wanted to make sure everything's okay first."

"Yeah, I'll keep my eyes peeled. Just goin' to get in an hour or two of diggin' before I go to work. It's good to be the boss!"

Jonathan couldn't believe the bad timing. Now he would have to stay. He couldn't take the chance that Andy would go into the north shaft and find Maggie. Damn! "Tell you what, Andy, I've got time, so I'll give you a hand. I can change my clothes before my client comes this afternoon."

"Ya sure ya wanna do that, Bear. Those are awful spiffy duds."

"The faster we get this dug out, the better."

"Ya got that right! This murder is gonna bring more attention to the mine."

Jonathan was going to have to burn his suit anyway. Between the grime and sweat, he'd have blood spatter to deal with. Pity, it was one of his favorites. He had tied Maggie up well, so she wasn't going anywhere. She would just have to keep till they were done. He and Andy walked together down the main shaft, their voices echoing eerily off the walls.

Chapter Thirty-two

"You have to believe me, Sheriff. Maggie will have confided in Jonathan, and now they've both gone missing. It has to be him! He could be killing her right now and you want me to repeat the story again? Fuck that!" Cher grabbed her purse and marched for the door. "You can arrest me or help me save my friend." Her grand exit was thwarted by the fact that the door was still locked from the outside. She knocked loudly at the door, which was promptly opened by Mike. She stormed past him and headed for the main entrance.

Artie pinched the bridge of his nose and sighed. He wouldn't even have time to grab some aspirin. As he walked out the door, he saw Cher by the roadside, trying to thumb a ride. This would have been more effective if there were any cars on the narrow street. He whistled for her and pointed to his car.

They got in the cruiser and headed for the motel. "I'm not going on a wild goose chase, Ms. Anderson. We need to rule out the possibility that she's safe in your room."

Within minutes they were at the motel. Maggie's car was missing from the parking lot, and they found her key card on the ground in front of the door. Cher dashed inside, calling over her shoulder, "I knew it!"

Cher rushed past the dogs, who were slavering with joy to see her. She checked the bathroom and closet.

"Not here. He'll have taken her to the mine. He could be dumping her body down one of the pit shafts right now!"

"Assuming that Jonathan is the killer, what makes you think he'll have taken her to the mine?"

Cher was not going to claim women's intuition to this man. He would laugh in her face. "He'll want to make sure that nobody else has found the gold, and he's already dumped one body there." Cher was wringing her hands, while Buddy jumped circles around her. "We'll bring the dogs. They'll be able to track her down."

Artie didn't have the will to argue, so he opened the back car door and the dogs leapt into the cruiser. He didn't expect to find anybody at the mine, but he wasn't going to let Cher out of his sight. He didn't need her running off after sending him on a fool's errand.

How long had it been since she'd heard the voices? A half hour? An hour? Probably longer. Her hands were finally free. She had dropped the rock several times, fighting a growing numbness in her fingers. She flexed her fingers now, willing the blood to return. Maggie fumbled with the knot on the gag, still hanging around her neck and flung it away. It only took her a moment to untie her ankles, but her feet had fallen asleep. While she waited for the feeling to return, she groped feverishly at her jeans pocket. She nearly swooned with relief when she felt her cigarette lighter. If she got out of here alive, she vowed never to leave home without her lighter. She stood tentatively—a little wobbly and aching from her toes to her hair. After being constrained in one position so long, movement sent shocks of pain from her neck down to her elbows.

She flicked her lighter and squinted at the blinding flare. The lighter did little to penetrate the blackness, but much to lift her spirits. She was in some sort of chamber with a few boxes, some rubber boots, and a scale like the ones she'd seen drug dealers use on *Cops*. There, sitting on one of the boxes was a lantern, glinting bright red in her feeble light. Her heart skipped a beat as she grabbed it and held it lovingly to her chest. She set it on the ground, lifted the globe, and lit the wick. It may look like an antique but it cast a comforting pool of light extending about five feet away from her. The chamber was not that big, but her light was low enough that she still couldn't quite make out the wall opposite her. She held the lantern high, as she walked around the chamber, searching for a way out of her prison. To her left she saw a gaping hole of deeper darkness, and realized that she had found the mine shaft.

She thought she could hear her heart echoing down the passageway as she felt her way along one solid reassuring wall. She wasn't sure how far she had gone, when she heard the voices again. This time they were closer.

They had dug out a couple of fair size nuggets, and Jonathan was anxious to get Andy away from the mine. "It's getting late. We should probably get out of here." Jonathan picked up his suit jacket and threw it over his arm, effectively hiding the chisel still in his hand. He picked up the gold nuggets and his lantern in the other hand.

"I reckon you're right, Bear. Time to get back to my day job."

They started up the shaft together in silence, until they reached the intersecting north shaft. Jonathan turned to Andy. "I'll go weigh the gold. See you back in town."

"Sure, Bear. I'll see ya."

Jonathan listened to Andy's retreating footsteps before entering the north shaft.

"That's her car!" Cher nearly shouted in Artie's ear as they pulled into the clearing near the mine entrance. "Please, God, let us be in time."

Artie was frankly surprised. He hadn't expected to find anybody at the mine. "That looks like Andy's truck parked next to it."

Just as he pulled the police cruiser to a stop in front of the mine entrance, he saw Andy squeezing past the chain link fence. He got out of the car, hand on his gun.

Cher burst from the car. "What have you done with her? Where is she?" She was letting the dogs out of the back as she shouted.

"Andy," Artie said calmly, "where's Jonathan?"

Andy looked confused, his eyes focused on the gun in Artie's hand. "I just left him in the mine. He was headed up the north spur."

Cher was fairly dancing in agitation as the dogs sniffed happily at the trees on the edge of the clearing.

"Was he alone?" Artie asked.

"Yeah. We was just doin' a little diggin'. He should be out in a minute."

Cher had pulled Artie's mag light out of the cruiser and was sprinting for the mine entrance, the dogs in hot pursuit.

Ah, hell! Artie thought, as he took off after her.

Chapter Thirty-three

As soon as she heard the voices, Maggie trimmed the wick on her lantern—just in time before she saw a soft glow of light farther down the shaft. Her heart was racing. For now, she was invisible, but she knew that the lantern light would penetrate far enough around Jonathan that he'd be able to make her out in the shadows. She wished that the shaft was about 10 feet wider than it was. Sticking out from the wall next to her was a rough-hewn support beam. If she were a half-starved super model, she might be able to hug the wall next to the beam tightly enough to have little exposed, but as she planted her chest as tight into the wall as possible, she was sure that her butt was sticking out about a mile.

Too much carrot cake, she thought as she fought back a sob.

She knew it was stupid to be facing the wall, but somehow she felt that if she couldn't see him, he wouldn't see her. *Lord, I'll quit smoking, I'll go to the gym, just please get me out of this.*

Her eyes were scrunched shut as she heard the steps nearly on top of her ... then continuing past.

She cautiously turned her head to watch Jonathan's back as he continued down the shaft. He was looking down as he walked. That was when she realized that she was still holding her breath. As soon as the glow of his lantern disappeared around a bend, she lit her lantern and looked down at herself. Her hands and her clothes were covered in gritty dust from rolling around on the mine floor. Even with the lantern on the ground right next to her legs, her jeans looked more gray than blue. She could only imagine the state of her backside. She had been all but invisible, blending into the wall.

She started running. At this point, she didn't care how much noise she was making. This was not a drill, she wasn't having an anxiety attack, but she was in full panic mode: no thought, just the overwhelming need to move. She couldn't tell if she heard footsteps behind her over the rushing of blood in her ears and the sound of her own ragged breathing. She refused to look back. She reached a junction, and stopped abruptly. She had no idea where she was or which way to turn. Now she could clearly hear footsteps behind her, running.

Right … right is always good. She started running again. A dark shape loomed up on her right and she nearly peed her pants. Her mind was able to register then—it was the cave entrance. *Dammit,* she was heading deeper into the mine. Hiding had worked once, she thought as she ducked down into the crevice. She wriggled through a few feet of low clearance in a natural tunnel, and she emerged into what must be an enormous cavern. She had to watch her feet as she made the best speed she could across the rocky cave floor. She hadn't gone fifty feet when she turned back to see a glow brightening the entrance, and Jonathan emerging. They stared at each other for a heartbeat, before she spun and ran full tilt. The stones here were smoother and easier going. Her lantern light sparked off ripples in a stream to her left. She heard Jonathan clattering along in the rough rocks. He was moving too fast, and she was getting a stitch in her side. Abruptly, the stream disappeared under a rock wall. She was at a dead end. She barely registered that there were thin wooden stakes laid out in a pattern on the ground with cheerful little orange flags attached.

She turned around in time to feel a fist connect with her left cheekbone. The blow knocked her off her feet. She lay sprawled on her back in a small pile of freshly turned earth. The lantern was no longer in her hand, and her vision was wavering in the dimmer glow of the single lamp. She could see his face. His lips were moving, but she could hear nothing over the roaring in her ears. Suddenly, he was on his knees, straddling her stomach. The look of hatred on his face was totally at odds with the handsome man they had met at the inn. The transformation rocked her and sent chills running down her spine. As his hands closed around her throat, stars exploded before her eyes. Lungs deprived of oxygen from running felt like they were now on fire. She writhed beneath him, trying to pry his fingers off her neck. No good. She spread her arms out to the side, looking for a rock, anything, when her hand connected with one of the stakes.

In a single desperate motion, she yanked the stake out of the soft earth and skimmed it between their bodies, before jamming it upward as hard as her failing strength allowed. It was the pointed end of the stake that impaled her attacker in the groin.

Jonathan rolled off her, howling. He curled up in a ball, clutching at himself, alternating between screams and gurgling noises. Maggie's body felt like lead as she fought for breath. She wanted to get up and run, but she could barely lift her head.

There was a wet sensation on her face, and she was able to recognize Buddy, happily giving her doggie kisses. Something was straddling her stomach, and she feared that Jonathan was getting back on top of her. Buddy's face filled her field of vision. She had to twist her head before she saw a black mass of fur where Jonathan had once been. Her sweet, timid Fluffy was standing protectively over her, facing the man who was now whimpering on the ground. Fluffy's teeth were bared; a frightening low growl from deep in his chest reverberated off the walls around them. He was suddenly all Rottweiller, and he meant business.

Cher pulled Buddy away from her face and knelt down beside her. She was crying and laughing. "It's a damn good thing you're alive, because you still owe me a package of hot dogs!"

Maggie tried to reassure her, but all that came out was a croaking noise. Her head was starting to clear as she saw the Sheriff on her other side, putting the cuffs on Jonathan. Cher shooed Fluffy off her, where he stood to one side and continued to glare at the man, cuffed and still rolling on the ground. Maggie lifted her hand and looked at the flag, grasped loosely in her fingers. There was blood on the end of the stake. Maggie gave a weak smile and a sigh of deep relief.

Chapter Thirty-four

A week had passed and Ted was still fussing over her. Normally Maggie didn't much like that, but after her near-death experience, the people she loved were more precious to her than ever. She could live with a little fussing. Her neck was still bruised and sore, so he had made her some grits for breakfast. She ate her grits while re-reading Cher's article in the *Post and Courier*. Cher had expanded her earlier version to give a better background on the story for a larger audience. The newspaper had snatched up the story and run it almost verbatim. They gave Cher a byline and an open invitation to send them any freelance stories for consideration.

They'd gotten a little drunk last night, so Cher had stayed in the guest room. She staggered into the kitchen now and smiled as she saw the paper.

Maggie's voice was still a little raspy. "Ummm! I'm in flavor country." She stroked the nicotine patch on her arm.

Cher laughed and stroked hers as well. "Hurry and finish your breakfast, darling, so we can get this damn walk out of the way."

"I'm not sure that I can walk today, sweetie. I think these spandex shorts are cutting off my circulation."

"Not buying it."

"I lost my pedometer."

"I caught you trying to flush it down the toilet last night after your second Margarita. What kind of walking buddy would I be if I let you drown the only piece of exercise equipment that you own?"

"What if Jeanine Stout is lurking outside waiting to ambush me again. Really, the woman is relentless."

"I hate to be the one to break it to you, darling, but you're already old news."

"Oh well," Maggie sighed, "with luck, maybe I'll sprain an ankle so we can get out of the book club next month."

"That's the spirit, darling!"

Cher poured herself a cup of coffee while Maggie finished her breakfast.

Elena burst through the kitchen door. "Mom, you'll never believe what happened!"

"You and George set a date?"

"Nah. We eloped last week while you were trying to get yourself killed."

"Damn! I was looking forward to showing up in one of those chiffon tents that mothers of the bride are supposed to wear."

"George got a promotion! He's going to be manager of the downtown Piggly Wiggly! He wants to move in with me to be closer to work!"

Maggie choked on her sip of coffee. She could have sworn some of it came out her nose.

Cher patted Maggie on the back and asked, "When is the baby due, darling?"

Elena knelt next to Maggie and took her hand as a new spasm of coughing overtook her. "Don't worry, Mom. I said no."

Maggie looked at the hand that used to be so tiny in hers. "Oh, thank God. I would never be able to visit you again, since I'm allergic to tofu and sprouts. I'm very happy for George."

"Cher, have you heard anything from Paul?" Elena asked as she straightened up and walked over to the coffee pot.

"He called yesterday. The department wasn't able to authenticate the jar, so there may be no way to prove his theory that the burial ground belongs to the Wind Clan. They might still be able to find some more conclusive evidence once they start the dig. That's assuming that they can get permits."

"The District Attorney called ... again." Maggie rolled her eyes. "It seems that the criminal justice system will grind to a halt unless he can get his deposition tomorrow. Seems they're reopening the murder investigation of Jonathan's wife. I asked the DA about that Andy fellow. He said that the only thing they could get him for would be trespassing, and even that would be a weak case, since the mine wasn't clearly posted and is part of the National Forest."

Elena whistled. "Does that mean he gets to keep all the gold he dug up?"

Cher answered. "Looks like it. The National Forest got the mineral rights once the mine played out, so he was legally allowed to dig. I'm writing a follow-up to the story. The Forest Service has closed the mine pending bids from different mining companies to lease the mineral rights. The University is petitioning for access to the burial site in the cave. We'll see how it plays out."

"So what mischief do you two have lined up for your next adventure?" Elena asked.

"We decided we need a break from sociopathic murderers, so we're going for a weekend in Savannah," Maggie answered. "The Marshall House is supposed to be one of the most haunted hotels in the country. Ted would go with us, but there's no dragging him away from the weekend games during football season."

"Then let me know when you're going so I can take time off from work. Somebody has to ride shotgun on you ladies and keep you out of trouble!"

Maggie looked around the kitchen. "Did anyone see where Ted went?"

Suddenly, they heard the roar of the lawn mower in the garage, followed by Ted's triumphant shout, "Huzzah! I am the Man!"

Acknowledgments

Books don't just happen. I couldn't have written *Box of Rocks* without the aid of some very special people. I'd like to thank my husband, Dave, who supported my crazy notion of becoming a writer, and who kept the coffee pot going. Special thanks to my dear friend, Katie Foryan, who never let me stop believing in myself. To my editors, Rosanne Dingli and Martin Rus, who volunteered their time to clean up my mistakes. To my wonderful readers: Norma Beishir, Karrin Johnson, Alexander Zoltai, Terri Sonoda, and Rebecca Gibson. Their suggestions and encouragement were invaluable. Thanks to Michael Brown of the Charleston Ghost Tour, Dr. Nichols of the Richland County Coroner's Office, and the McCormick Police Department. Cover art by El Kartün,

www.elkartun.zirculomarketing.com

About the Author

Despite the best efforts of the psychiatric community, Karla Telega has unleashed her first book on society with *Box of Rocks.* She is a graduate of hot flashes who writes mysteries, humor, and a killer Christmas letter. She lives with her husband in South Carolina, where she enjoys reading, watching football, and walking her dog. You can share adventures in aging on her humor blog, or contact her at www.telegatales.com

www.ingramcontent.com/pod-product-compliance
Lightning Source LLC
Chambersburg PA
CBHW071309170626
46809CB00001B/384

* 9 7 8 0 6 1 5 7 2 5 6 2 8 *